PRAISE FOR ELLEN FELD'S BOOK *ANNIE!*

"The story shows strong examples of good horse care and kind handling as well as promoting the value of careful preparation to gain successful results. This wonderful book will have readers seeking all Ellen Feld's books if they haven't already read them."

> —Caryn Sappelli,
> *The United States Pony Clubs, Inc.*

"*Annie* is more than just a story about winning show competitions for horses. It's about how to bond with and treat horses, any animal for that matter, and how that brings out the best in all involved. Even if you've never ridden a horse, you'll wind up wanting to try after reading this sensitive and tender novel, and you will definitely be even more interested in finding out more about this particular breed of proud, talented Morgan Horses! Exquisite! Wonderful!"

> —Viviane Crystal,
> *Crystal Reviews*

"No doubt about it, I'm simply captivated by Ellen Feld's Morgan Horse series. She really knows about horses and, without trying to be trite, is the horse whisperer of the teen horse set."

> —Deb Fowler,
> *Roundtable Reviews*

"*Annie* is an absolutely fabulous book! Ellen Feld has a thorough knowledge of horses and pleasure riding and I simply loved this book!"

> —Brianne Plach,
> *Reader Views*

ANNIE:
The Mysterious Morgan Horse

THE MORGAN HORSE SERIES
BY ELLEN F. FELD
Read Them All!

Blackjack: Dreaming of a Morgan Horse

ISBN 978-0-9709002-8-9

An International Reading Association— Children's Book Council "Children's Choices" Selection

"Mrs. Feld has a true gift in capturing the imagination and engaging the reader. It isn't always easy to find a book that will be read willingly by pre-teens! Kudos to Mrs. Feld on her delightful *Morgan Horse* series."

— Jenefer Igarashi, Senior Editor,
The Old Schoolhouse Magazine

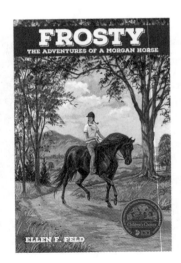

Frosty: The Adventures of a Morgan Horse

ISBN 978-0-9831138-6-7

An International Reading Association— Children's Book Council "Children's Choices" Selection

"... a thoroughly delightful novel for young readers about a girl and her relationship with powerful and noble animals ... Frosty is a story to be cherished by horse lovers of all ages."

—*Midwest Book Review*

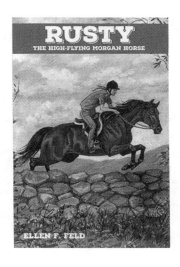

Rusty: The High-Flying Morgan Horse

ISBN 978-0-9831138-2-9

A Parent to Parent Adding Wisdom Award Winner

"Through her choice words and obvious first-hand knowledge, Ellen Feld conveys to the reader that special connection a girl has with her horse. A thoroughly enjoyable read—I only wish it had been published when I was a teenager!"

—Cindy Mark, Editor, *Horses All*

Robin: The Lovable Morgan Horse

ISBN 978-0-9709002-5-8

A Parent to Parent Adding Wisdom Award Winner

"Feld uses plenty of conflict on many levels, a string of obstacles, and the characters' solutions to craft a very interesting story with a quick pace. We rated this book five hearts."

—Bob Spear, *Heartland Reviews*

Annie: The Mysterious Morgan Horse

ISBN 978-0-9709002-9-6

A Moonbeam Children's Book Award Winner and A Reader Views Literary Award Winner

"Annie combines an exciting story with a lot of practical information. It's another blue-ribbon winner from author Ellen Feld!"

—*Horsemen's Yankee Pedlar*

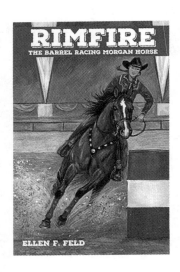

Rimfire: The Barrel Racing Morgan Horse

ISBN 978-0-9709002-1-0

Selected as the Best New Book for 2010 by Tack 'n Togs Magazine

"Rimfire brings the exciting world of barrel racing to life in a fun and delightful way! A great book for our youth and a valuable reminder that quitters never win and winners never quit."

—Martha Josey, *AQHA, WPRA, NBHA World Champion, Olympic Medalist, Hall of Fame*

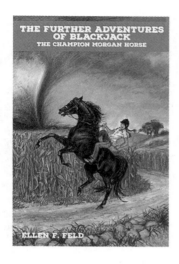

The Further Adventures of Blackjack: The Champion Morgan Horse

ISBN 978-0-9831138-5-0

The Further Adventures of Blackjack "... has excitement, suspense, and a surprise ending, all coming together with a satisfying understanding of horses. It is another blue-ribbon winner from a talented author."

—Nancy Norton, Editor,
Horse & Academy Magazine

Meet the Morgans

ISBN 978-0-9831138-4-3

The perfect companion book to the popular *Morgan Horse* series. With over 50 photos of the real horses behind the books, readers will get an inside look at the Morgans who inspired the series.

ALSO FROM WILLOW BEND PUBLISHING

Blackjack: The Magical Morgan Horse

ISBN: 978-0-9831138-6-7

A girl, a horse, and some magical stardust - sometimes dreams really do come true...

Shadow: The Curious Morgan Horse

ISBN 978-0-9831138-3-6

A USA Book News Best Books Award Winner

"You are guaranteed to delight in this story of a young, adventurous foal. Feld is a talented, creative, artistic writer who clearly loves her topic of horses. Absolutely delightful!"

—Viviane Crystal, *Crystal Reviews*

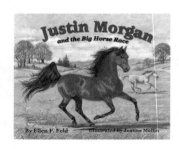

Justin Morgan and the Big Horse Race

ISBN 978-0-9831138-1-2

"A beautiful story with magnificent drawings that's pure entertainment."

—Amy Lignor, *Feathered Quill Book Reviews*

Pidgy's Surprise

ISBN 978-0-9831138-0-5

"Written and fantastically illustrated by famed equine artist Jeanne Mellin, this re-release of a popular story from the 1950's offers a heart-felt story of a young girl and her discovery of the path of her dreams."

—*BookPleasures.com*

What Can I Do?
A Donkey-Donk Story

ISBN: 978-0-9831138-7-4

"If you are searching for a picture book to read to your homeschooler or class that will illicit smiles, peels of laughter, and giggles, then look no further."

—*Valerie Schuetta, M.Ed., Classroom Reviews*

What Does A Police Horse Do?

ISBN 978-0-9831138-9-8

Meet Liam - a police horse with the Lancaster, PA Mounted Police Unit. Follow along with this very special horse to learn just what a police horse does every day.

ANNIE:

The Mysterious Morgan Horse

Ellen F. Feld

Willow Bend Publishing
Goshen, MA 01032

Published by Willow Bend Publishing

Illustrated by Jeanne Mellin
Cover design by 8 Create Graphic Design
Book design by Linda Mahoney, LM Design
Composition by Susan Leonard

Library of Congress Catalog Card Number: 2007931431
ISBN: 978-0-9709002-9-6

Direct inquiries to:
Willow Bend Publishing
P.O. Box 304
Goshen, MA 01032
www.willowbendpublishing.com

Printed in the United States of America

10   9   8   7   6   5   4

To Nicholas

It is so exciting to see you and Rimfire
growing up together.
Whether you decide to enter the show ring or
simply enjoy trail rides with your new horse,
I know you'll have a blast.

Love always, Mom

ACKNOWLEDGMENTS

I would like to thank Jeanne Mellin for good-naturedly taking on yet another project and creating some amazing artwork for this book. Her beautiful pictures add so much to my story. Thanks to Grant D. Myhre B.S., D.V.M. for his thorough review of the medical portions of the text, and for the wonderful care he and his staff gave the real Rerun when she visited his clinic. Dr. Michelle G. Hutchinson of Wordhelper Editing Services has once again provided a careful review of the text and without her help I'd be lost. Anne Brown very willingly put up with countless phone calls to verify historical aspects of the story and has always been a great source of Morgan facts.

*The chestnut horse, upset and confused, continued to
toss her head as she jigged down the rail.*

A VERY BAD HORSE SHOW

"**W**alk, Polly, walk," snarled the rider in a whispered voice. He snapped the reins harshly several times in an effort to slow the pretty Morgan mare to a walk. But the chestnut horse, upset and confused, continued to toss her head as she jigged down the rail. The bouncy movement, a mix of a walk and a trot, threw the rider around in the saddle. Polly's ears were pinned back and she swished her tail constantly. It was not a pleasant sight.

The rider grew more and more annoyed at his horse. His body became tense as he once again pulled back on the reins. Polly was afraid. She could feel her rider's anger and grew more anxious. The heavy-handed rider was hurting the frightened mare's mouth. "I said walk!" he whispered to his horse in a spiteful voice. He didn't want anybody to hear him, especially the judge.

While horse and rider fought, the judge, standing in center ring, carefully watched them. Noting the horse's uneasiness, the judge wrote something on his notepad and then looked elsewhere.

"Lope, all lope," came the order over the loudspeakers.

Fifteen Morgan Horses all decked out in fancy western show attire, with silver oozing from every part of their saddles and bridles, calmly broke into a relaxed, slow lope, the western version of a canter.

The sixteenth horse, Polly, jumped up with her front end and landed hard as she stumbled into a lope. Her head flew high into the air, mouth gaping open as her rider jerked hard on the bit. He had tightened the reins so much that the poor mare was forced to open her mouth to try and get away from the pain. She swung her tail violently as she cantered sideways down the rail. The judge, who had been watching a lovely bay mare in front of Polly, now focused his attention on the chestnut mare.

Polly was a very pretty horse with a long, flowing mane and tail, both colored light brown with streaks of red. Her body was a little darker, which made her left hind sock, shaped like a small triangle, and white hoof stand out. She had a big, bold star on her forehead and a little white snip of hair and pink skin between her nostrils. Her fancy western saddle had silver on every flat surface and the bridle reins were wrapped in the shiny metal too. The headstall, the portion of the bridle that ran along the side of Polly's head, had so much silver on it that it was hard to see any leather underneath. The bit, too, was incredibly ornate, with a fancy floral design. Unfortunately, the part of the bit that ran through Polly's mouth, the section nobody could see, was an extremely severe device. With a little pressure on the reins, it could cause a lot of pain. Polly knew this all too well as she tossed her head, desperately trying to get away from the discomfort. The judge watched Polly struggle with her rider, but he only needed a moment to determine the mare wouldn't place in his ring. He quickly turned to watch another horse.

The horses loped twice around the ring while the judge carefully observed them. Then, satisfied that he had seen enough, he called for a walk. Polly once again refused to walk, instead prancing down the rail. "Kevin! Make her walk!" commanded a middle-aged man standing on the outside of the ring.

"I'm trying, Jim!" snapped the rider in reply. "She won't listen to me."

"Line up in center ring," ordered a voice over the loudspeakers. Kevin, Polly's rider, had thought the command would never come. He hated riding the unruly mare and was glad the class was over.

Polly jigged into the middle of the ring and came to a stop between two other mares. The other horses calmly waited as the judge slowly made his way down the line. Polly, however, refused to stand still. She pawed at the ground, swished her tail, and then moved her hind end from side to side. Kevin yanked the reins, trying to get the horse to stop moving.

Instead, the upset Morgan backed up several steps. In response, Kevin kicked his horse hard with the heels of his western boots.

Polly gasped as her rider's heels dug deeply into her sides. She leapt into the air and landed several feet ahead of where she had stood. The two riders on either side of Kevin gave him a nasty look. Their horses were getting upset by Polly's bad behavior. Kevin ignored them as he again pulled back tightly on the reins. This time, Polly turned her rump to the left and bumped into the horse next to her. That horse pinned her ears at Polly but continued to stand still. It was at that moment that the judge passed Polly.

Kevin, seeing the official, grew even angrier at his horse, and as soon as the judge moved away, he kicked Polly again. Polly had nowhere to go but up. She threw her front legs into the air as her head went back, nose flying outward. Jumping forward, she landed hard and then trotted several steps. Thinking quickly, Kevin guided Polly to the far end of the ring, around the horses and back into place. As he asked his horse to stop, the order came to retire. All the riders knew this meant the judge had turned in his scorecard and the class was over. All the riders went to the far end of the ring to patiently wait to hear the placings for the class.

Kevin followed the crowd but again, his horse refused to quietly wait. He was forced to walk his horse nonstop in a small, tight circle. Looking up, he saw his boss, Jim Spencer, standing by the rail. The man didn't look happy. Kevin knew as soon as the class was over, Mr. Spencer was going to yell at him for the bad ride. Taking his aggravation out on Polly, Kevin pulled hard on the reins as he kicked his horse. "I said walk!" he growled.

"We have the winners for class 52, Western Pleasure Mare and Gelding," boomed the speakers. "In first place is number 359, Grand Creek Pioneer, owned and ridden by John Keesher."

Kevin watched as the winner jogged slowly into center ring to receive his blue ribbon. Polly, still tossing her head, was forced to walk in tight little circles as the rest of the ribbons were handed out. Then, once the eighth place winner was announced, Kevin turned his horse toward the gate and exited the ring. Guiding the horse about twenty feet from the ring, he stopped and waited for Mr. Spencer. Polly finally stood still.

Kevin was not looking forward to what his boss was going to say. Within moments, Mr. Spencer came storming over to them. He was a grumpy looking man in his mid-forties, with brown hair that had started to turn gray around the edges. He was wearing a long-sleeve white cotton shirt, jeans, and work boots. There was a crop sticking out of his back pocket, which had been used many times on Polly. Seeing him and his whip frightened the mare who knew too well what Mr. Spencer was capable of doing. "I told you to walk in that ring," shouted Mr. Spencer.

"I tried, Jim, but she wouldn't listen to me," replied Kevin, trying to defend himself. Kevin Jones was a handsome young man in his early twenties. He had grown up in a city but had never enjoyed living in a place surrounded by buildings and pavement. When he graduated from high school, Kevin had decided that he wanted to live in the country and needed to find a job. After spending several months searching for the right position, with no horse experience at all, he started working as a groom for Mr. Spencer. He loved living in the country but really didn't like working with horses. But with no other education, he felt he had few choices, so he decided to make his living with the often annoying animals. Now, five years later, he was Mr. Spencer's assistant trainer.

"This mare isn't going to make a fool of me," announced Mr. Spencer. "Take her out in the back field where nobody can see you, and ride her hard. Then I want you to ride her hard again tomorrow. Really hard, Kevin. I want her lathered up with sweat. That way, by Friday, for her championship class, she'll be better. Mrs. Clayburg will be here for that class."

"Mrs. Clayburg?" asked a worried Kevin. He knew the woman owned the chestnut mare along with four other horses under Mr. Spencer's care. It was very important that they impress her.

"Yes," replied Mr. Spencer, "and you know how essential it is that this horse does well on Friday."

"Of course," agreed the young rider. "Don't worry, Jim, I'll get her going."

"Good. You've got two days to get her to behave. How are you going to make her walk?"

"I'll work her in the field," said Kevin, "running her until she's too tired to keep going. After a good, long run Polly will want to walk."

"That sounds perfect. Now go work her hard. I don't want this mare thinking she can get away with her obnoxious behavior."

Kevin clucked and at the same time dug his heels into Polly's side. The mare immediately responded by breaking into a nervous trot. They moved past the warm up arena, the food vendors, and beyond the trucks and horse trailers to a grassy field that was separated from the nearby highway by a six-foot tall chain-link fence. Kevin was relieved to find the area vacant. He didn't want to share the space, nor did he want his actions viewed by nosey onlookers. He suspected the workout wouldn't be viewed favorably by others; he knew Polly would finish the training period breathing heavily and sweating profusely.

"Trot, mare, trot," Kevin ordered as the Morgan continued to prance. When showing in a western class, a rider is only allowed to use one hand on the reins. The other hand must never be used to guide the horse. But now that they were out of the show ring, Kevin could use both hands, so he took full advantage of the power of his arms to slow the horse. "Not so fast," he snarled. But Polly knew her rider was angry and tense and it caused the frightened mare to go even faster. "Fine," growled Kevin. "You want to go fast, huh? I'll give you fast," and he kicked Polly hard. "Lope, you stubborn mare."

Polly jumped into a lope and continued to increase her speed. She tried to free herself from the pain of the bit by tossing her head forward, but the tight reins prevented any head movement. Unable to extend her head, she instead bounced her body up and down. It was the only thing she could do. Kevin, in response, flopped all over the place. He was thrown forward and back, and every time he fell backwards, he landed hard on Polly's back. "Don't stop, you stupid horse," ordered Kevin when he felt Polly beginning to slow down. "You'll be begging to go slow by the time I finish with you," he laughed.

Several minutes went by and still the pair was flying around the field. Polly had broken into a sweat, and there was a white, foamy lather between her back legs. She was tired and wanted to stop but her rider wouldn't let her. Every time she started to slow down, she received a hard kick on her sides. Soon her neck was soaked with sweat and there too, lather was beginning to accumulate.

Kevin continued to jab the reins hard until a trickle of blood started flowing from one side of Polly's mouth. "Had enough?" he asked the horse.

Polly was too tired to fight now and instead, stumbled and almost fell. Falling forward, the rider grabbed the mare's mane with both hands to keep himself in the saddle. Regaining his balance, he immediately stuck his heels into Polly's side again. "That'll teach you," he scolded.

Finally, as Polly's nostrils flared, trying to get enough air into her lungs, she was asked to stop. Coming to a quick halt was the worst thing a horse should do after such a strenuous workout. The horse needed to be brought slowly down, first by trotting, then by walking. But Kevin either didn't care or didn't know.

Polly stood perfectly still, head hanging down, steam flowing up from her neck into the afternoon air. Her sides heaved in and out so much that Kevin could easily feel the motion. The blanket underneath the bulky western saddle was drenched with sweat. The young trainer had a look of pleasant satisfaction on his face. He had taught the annoying horse a lesson.

After several minutes, a young woman led a yearling colt into the field. She smiled at Kevin but quickly turned away when she got a closer look at the exhausted horse. Leading the colt to a far corner, she snapped a lunge line onto the youngster's halter, let out about fifteen feet of the rope, and asked the horse to trot around her. The bay colt had a gleeful, playful look to him; he was happy to be out of his stall and had a lot of pent-up energy he needed to release. Letting out a loud squeal, he kicked up his heels and bolted into a flurry of motion. The sound startled Polly who glanced over at the baby but then she turned away. She was too tired to care.

Kevin decided the lesson was over. Kicking Polly, he turned the horse toward the barn. With her head dragging low, Polly slowly made her way to the stabling area. Kevin slid off the mare and handed the reins to Kelly, one of two grooms who worked for Mr. Spencer. "Cool her off," he commanded, without ever looking at Polly or Kelly.

Kelly, a slender twenty-year-old woman with blonde hair and dirty clothes, obediently took the reins from Kevin and led Polly to a grooming stall. The instant Kelly removed Polly's saddle and blanket, a mountain of steam rolled off the mare's back. The blanket was soaked with sweat and would need a good cleaning before it could be used in the show ring again. Kelly had seen so many horses drenched in sweat, heads hanging low, and breathing heavily, return from workouts with Kevin or Mr. Spencer, that she actually thought it was the way all trainers worked their horses. The young groom next replaced the fancy show bridle with an old blue nylon halter. As the halter was slid onto the mare, the weary horse tried to rub her head on Kelly's arm. Polly received a quick slap for her actions. "Cut that out," warned the groom. Then Kelly began the long job of cooling off the horse.

Twenty minutes later Kelly was still walking Polly. The warm summer temperature made it difficult for the mare's body to expel the extra heat. Still, her breathing had returned to normal and the horse was starting to feel better. "You still walking that horse?" came a voice from behind Kelly.

"Yeah," she replied, recognizing the voice of Mr. Spencer. "She's real hot."

"Well, put her away. Domino's class is this afternoon and you've got to start getting him ready."

"Domino?" asked the groom.

"Yes, you heard me. Domino," snapped Mr. Spencer.

Kelly knew that Domino, a dark bay Morgan stallion, was Mr. Spencer's top show horse. Like Polly, he belonged to Mrs. Clayburg, but unlike the mare, Domino frequently won top honors at the shows he attended. He was a fancy, high-stepping park horse who also refused to walk. But since he was shown in park classes, where few horses performed a flat-footed walk and instead moved in a slow, animated trot when asked to walk, Domino's poor behavior was often misinterpreted. The handsome stallion, once a bold, happy show horse, had changed when he was placed in the care of Mr. Spencer. Now he too, feared the abusive trainer.

Knowing that Mr. Spencer would yell at her if she didn't respond immediately, Kelly acted quickly. She knew the mare needed more care before being put away, but the groom didn't want to get fired. She obediently put Polly back in her stall and turned her attention to Domino.

The day before Polly's championship class, Kevin had worked the mare incredibly hard. He had taken her back to the open field near the highway in the morning and had run the mare until she could hardly breathe. Head dragging, the horse finally walked without jigging. Believing it was the only way to get the mare to go properly, Kevin took Polly back to the field the morning of her class. Again, he worked her until she was drenched in sweat and having trouble breathing. But by the time Mrs. Clayburg arrived, the mare had been completely cooled off. The wealthy owner would never know what her horse was going through.

Polly was standing outside her stall, secured with cross ties that ran between her stall and an outside pole. Two other horses stood in similar fashion further down the barn aisle. "Has Domino gone yet?" asked the plump, gray-haired woman as she walked past Polly, completely ignoring the mare.

"No, ma'am," respectfully replied Kevin as he led the handsome stallion out of the grooming stall. "His class is in about 15 minutes."

"Good," said Mrs. Clayburg as she ran her hand through her short hair. "Mr. Spencer told me over the phone that the horse won a second. He expects

Domino to win the championship today and I want to see it." She wore a brightly colored dress and a long pearl necklace that hung limply down toward her plump belly. With high-heeled shoes, nylons, and a lacy shawl hanging loosely around her shoulders, Mrs. Clayburg was not dressed for the dusty environment of a horse show. "Do I have any other horses going today? I thought you said one of my mares was showing."

"Yes, that's correct, Mrs. Clayburg. Polly is going shortly after Domino," answered Kevin.

"Where is she?"

"She's right behind you, ma'am. You walked past her when you arrived."

"Oh," said Mrs. Clayburg, as she turned and looked at Polly. "I didn't recognize her; she looks so lovely," she said as she gave the mare a gentle pat. "Has she shown yet this week?"

Before Kevin could answer, Mr. Spencer walked up from behind him and answered Mrs. Clayburg. "The mare went in her qualifying class and had a real good go," he said, his lie obvious to Kevin and the two grooms who were working nearby.

"So what ribbon did she get?"

"The judge was blind," said Mr. Spencer, adding to his lie. "He's only judged a few shows and obviously has no idea how to pin a class. I can't believe some of the placings—"

"What color?" interrupted Mrs. Clayburg.

"She didn't pin," admitted Mr. Spencer. "She should have placed in the top three, but she didn't. But don't worry; the mare should do well today. Now, I've got to get ready to show Domino. Why don't you head up to the ring, find your box seat, and enjoy the show?"

"Yes, I think that's a good idea. I'll see you after my horses' classes," said Mrs. Clayburg as she turned and walked away.

With only three horses showing in the park saddle championship, Domino was guaranteed a top ribbon. His two competitors were the same horses he had shown against earlier in the week, and the class turned out to be a repeat of their earlier meeting. Another bay stallion, the winner of the previous class, had a fabulous headset, high-stepping action, and perfect manners. Domino, although his action was equal to the winner's, threw his head around, flattened his ears, and fought with his rider, Mr. Spencer. But the final horse refused to pick up the canter, so the judge was forced to place him third. Because it was the championship, Domino's second place ribbon made him the reserve champion in the park saddle division.

Mrs. Clayburg didn't know what her horse had done wrong. She simply thought her stallion was the prettiest horse in the ring, and therefore, he should have won. When she met Mr. Spencer at the barn after the class, she repeated her thoughts to him. "You're absolutely right," agreed Mr. Spencer.

"Domino was definitely the best horse in that class. But like I told you before, the judge at this show doesn't know what he's doing. He's blind. I know a lot of people saw that class, and they know Domino should have won too."

Feeling better now that she thought Domino's second place ribbon was the judge's fault, Mrs. Clayburg headed back to her box seat to watch Polly's class. Ten minutes later, Polly slowly jogged into the ring along with ten other horses. After the exhausting workout of the morning, the mare was too tired to fight Kevin. Her head hung low, too low for a Morgan western pleasure horse. When the walk was called, the horse obediently slowed to a walk. Her lope was rough, but the fight was gone. This time, when the judge watched Polly, there was no jigging down the rail. But the judge could see that the mare had no spark, no pleasure at being shown, no eagerness to display her talents. That was not the look he wanted in his winner.

When the class was pinned, Polly trotted out of the ring with a brown ribbon, eighth place. She was the lowest placing horse to get a ribbon. Two horses, each with major blunders, did not receive a ribbon. Mr. Spencer was furious. In his eyes, the mare had performed well. He did not understand the finer points of judging and why a horse who managed to behave would still place so low. He stormed over to the gate where Kevin and Polly were waiting. "That crappy judge," steamed Mr. Spencer. "He wouldn't know a good horse if it ran him over!"

Kevin, too, was upset. He took it out on Polly by yanking on the reins. In response, the Morgan threw her head up in the air, mouth gaping open. Kevin then kicked the mare and headed back to the barn with Mr. Spencer walking beside them. As they traveled, they tried to come up with an excuse for Mrs. Clayburg. They needed to explain why her horse had pinned so low.

FIRE!

By the time Mrs. Clayburg arrived at the barn, Kevin and Mr. Spencer had developed a plan. Taking turns, they would explain that the judge preferred high-strung, ill-mannered western horses. They knew their client, with almost no knowledge of the horse world, would believe whatever they said.

The scheme worked. With both trainers adding their opinions, Mrs. Clayburg was easily convinced the poor placing was the fault of the judge, not of the mare's bad training. "But if the mare won't win any blue ribbons, I don't know if I want to keep her," admitted the woman.

Kevin would love seeing Polly sold. He hated the mare and hated working her. But he knew that Mr. Spencer would be furious if he lost the training fees that Mrs. Clayburg sent each month. Kevin, therefore, did his best to convince her that the mare was worth keeping. With his boss listening closely, Kevin started his story. "You know, Mrs. Clayburg," he began, "the mare has come a long way since we got her two years ago. She's going to be a champion, I can tell. I'm sure you know that the best horses take several years before they start winning. You'll see, by next year, I'm willing to bet your mare wins plenty of blues."

Once he was satisfied that Mrs. Clayburg was sold on the idea of keeping her mare in training, Mr. Spencer wanted an excuse to get away from the woman. "Kelly," he barked, turning his attention to his groom, "is Blackjack ready yet?"

"You mean Dudley?" replied Kelly, who had been brushing a horse on the cross ties several feet away from the conversation. The grooms had nicknamed the handsome black stallion Dudley soon after his arrival at the barn. They hated the mean-spirited stallion and thought the name made the horse sound less threatening.

"Yes," answered Mr. Spencer, obviously very annoyed. "Dudley. Blackjack. Whatever you call him. Is he ready yet?"

"I haven't done anything with him."

"What?" shouted the irritated trainer. "Excuse me, Mrs. Clayburg. I've got a horse showing soon that hasn't even been groomed yet." Turning away, Mr. Spencer stormed over to Kelly. "I told you this morning I wanted that horse ready to go by noon."

"I know, Mr. Spencer," meekly replied the groom, "but I'm afraid of Blackjack. He's vicious."

"Oh, grow up," scolded Mr. Spencer. "If you ever want to be a trainer, you have to deal with obnoxious horses. That black stallion is spoiled rotten from his previous owner. I'll straighten him out."

Grabbing the whip from his back pocket, the irritated trainer headed to a stall on the far end of the barn. Polly, meanwhile, received a pat from her owner, the first show of affection the mare had seen in a very long time. Mrs. Clayburg then rushed off; she had a lunch meeting with several friends in half an hour. As soon as her owner left, Polly was returned to her stall. The show was over for her.

The following day, the show horses returned to Mr. Spencer's training facility. Polly was the last horse to be unloaded from the large van the horses traveled in. Eager to get out of the dark confines of her traveling stall, the mare repeatedly pawed. "Oh, stop that," grumbled Tammy, the other groom employed by Mr. Spencer. The young woman was tired and dirty, and desperately wanted a shower. She had no patience for horses today. "I'm not paid enough to put up with spoiled horses," Tammy told the mare. Looking around, she saw that all the other horses were off the van, so she untied Polly and led her down the long ramp to the ground. "Where do you want her?" Tammy asked Mr. Spencer.

"Um . . ." paused Mr. Spencer as he turned to look at Polly, "I don't want that mare up here. She won't be showing again until next year, and I don't plan on working her much over the winter, so bring her down to the lower barn."

"Okay," said Tammy as she led Polly away.

The upper barn was reserved for show horses in active training, while the lower barn was used for horses who were not worked on a regular basis. In contrast to the upper barn, which was a relatively clean and brightly lit building, the lower barn was an ancient structure that was falling apart. It was dark and musty, and most of the glass in the small windows had long ago been replaced by plywood. Each stall had once had a back door that had opened to a small run so the horses could go in and out whenever they wanted. But those doors had fallen off years ago, and like the windows, Mr. Spencer had them replaced with cheap pieces of plywood. The floor was uneven, the stalls small, the wooden beams holding up the roof were sagging, and the floor of the hayloft had numerous holes where the wood had rotted away.

Many of the horses kept in the lower barn were owned by clients paying hefty training fees. Before those owners came to visit, they were required to call Mr. Spencer, presumably to ensure that the trainer would be home when they arrived. But Mr. Spencer had another reason. Once he received a call, he would have the animal moved temporarily to the upper barn and the owner would then think, falsely, that his horse lived in the brightly lit upper barn. Most of these people didn't even know the lower barn existed.

As Tammy led Polly down the narrow aisle of the barn, she glanced at each stall, looking for an empty one. It was a ten-stall barn, five stalls on each side, and there were usually one or two vacant. Looking into one, Tammy saw Blackjack, the handsome Morgan stallion owned by Mr. Casey. *Blackjack is a pretty horse, but he's downright mean*, thought Tammy. How Mr. Spencer put up with such a vicious horse she didn't know. The stallion had been awful at the show, striking at another horse in his pleasure class and getting excused from the ring. Mr. Spencer had been furious, and the punishment the horse had received once he was taken away from the crowds had been severe. Now Blackjack was quietly eating a moldy flake of hay in the back of his stall. Tammy wondered what was next for the stallion. Would he ever be shown again?

Tammy found a free stall next to Blackjack's. "Get in here," the groom said. It was the last stall in the barn and was the darkest spot in the building.

Slipping the mare's halter off and shutting the door as she exited, Tammy looked around for a bale of hay. Unable to find any and knowing that the only hay was up in the loft, the young woman decided the horse could wait until dinnertime. "I'm not climbing up into the loft now," Tammy said as she tossed Polly's halter down onto the dirt floor and walked away.

For the next several weeks, Polly stood quietly in her stall. She was not turned out in a pasture to run and play, and the only time she saw a person was when Tammy or Kelly cleaned her stall or fed her. The mare was lonely and bored, and spent most of her time chewing the wood planks that surrounded her.

As time went by, fewer and fewer horses were kept in the lower barn. Many owners had decided to bring their horses home for the winter, perhaps hoping that several months of rest would help improve the animals' performances the following show season. Eventually, the only other horse in the barn was Blackjack. Both Polly and Blackjack were owned by clients who lived too far away to make frequent visits.

Meanwhile, Mr. Spencer, Kevin, and the grooms were kept busy caring for the animals in the upper barn where there was still plenty of activity. New horses were arriving to be trained over the winter, while the few successful show horses, the ones who somehow managed to perform under Mr. Spencer's stern hand, were kept in this nicer barn.

On a rainy, cold Saturday morning in mid-September, Mr. Spencer came storming into the lower barn, whip in hand. Polly recognized the thump-thump of Mr. Spencer's walk. Fearing the trainer was going to do something to her, the frightened mare huddled at the back of her stall. "Finally got your owner to agree with me," growled the man. "I won't have to put up with your crap anymore, you stupid horse."

Polly heard Blackjack's stall door open. "Get over here you miserable creature," shouted Mr. Spencer, as he whacked the whip on the door.

"I've got the tranquilizer," said Kelly, entering the barn.

"I told you to pack it in the truck. We can't tranquilize him here; it'll wear off before the auction. It has to be done after we get to the Fall Consignment Sale. Don't you know anything?"

"Sorry, Mr. Spencer."

After a few minutes of struggling with the stallion, Mr. Spencer got the halter on the horse and led the animal away. It would be the last time Polly saw Blackjack for a very long time. But they would meet again.

That evening, Polly patiently waited for her dinner. However, as the barn grew dark, nobody came. Mr. Spencer had taken Blackjack to an auction while the rest of the staff took the day off. Whoever was supposed to feed must have forgotten.

As time passed, Polly grew increasingly hungry. A smell slowly began to drift to her nostrils, but the mare immediately knew it wasn't food. Something was wrong; that smell meant danger. Polly whinnied but there was no answer. She started to pace around her stall. Stopping occasionally, she would paw through the dirty sawdust, look around in the dark, and then begin to pace again.

The electrical wires in the old barn had been in use for years. They hung down low in many places, especially up in the hayloft, and the many rats in the barn enjoyed chewing them. A particularly fat rat had concentrated his efforts that day on one spot where a wire was surrounded by old, dusty hay bales. The rat enjoyed the sense of security from all the hay.

The switch in the barn was frequently left on by the lazy grooms. It didn't take long for the rat to chew through the outer plastic coating and begin chewing on the copper wire. Suddenly the wire sparked. The rat jumped in fear and scurried away, but the spark ignited the hay, and within minutes a small fire had started.

The dry hay went up in flames in a flash. Soon the fire had spread to the ancient frame of the hayloft and then through the floorboards to the stalls below. Within minutes the whole barn was ablaze.

Polly was frantic. The fire hadn't reached her stall yet, but she could feel the heat and knew there was danger approaching. She squealed and hit her door with a hoof. She wanted to get out of the barn.

"Fire!" screamed Kevin as he dashed from his truck. He had been out with friends and forgotten to feed the horses. Arriving late, he was horrified to see the lower barn in flames. Without a moment's hesitation, he ran to the barn and into the crumbling building. It was hard to see with all the smoke, but Kevin had been in the barn so many times he was able to make his way without too much difficulty. He only stumbled once but quickly regained his footing as he dodged the hot flames.

Arriving at Polly's stall, he felt around the door for her halter, but Kelly had tossed it on the floor, so it was hard to find. Kevin grew anxious as he searched while the flames drew closer. "Come on," he yelled to himself, "where is it?" Kevin felt along the wall, and as he moved, his foot hit the halter. Bending down, he madly grabbed the halter and slipped through the door. But the horse didn't understand he was trying to save her; she could only sense his hysterical mood. The mare, therefore, fought his attempts to get the halter on her head. It took several minutes for Kevin to win the battle. By that time, the fire had spread down the aisle. They were trapped!

Kevin started to exit the stall but he immediately saw that the fire had engulfed the barn. How could they escape? The trainer's heart raced as he stumbled through the stall, pounding on the walls, desperately searching for a way out. Hitting the back wall, Kevin realized it was just a thin piece of plywood. It was the plywood that had been nailed on to cover up the exit to the outside pen. Grabbing madly at the plywood, Kevin pulled with all his strength. When the makeshift wall refused to budge, Kevin moved his fingers lower, trying to find a spot where the nails had been removed.

Fortunately, Polly had chewed much of the door panel during her confinement in the stall, and there were several areas where the plywood was no longer attached to the wall. Finding such a spot, Kevin pulled with all his might. As he grunted, he continued to pull, knowing this was now the only way out of the burning barn. "Come on," he pleaded. "Move, you stupid door. Move!"

The plywood began to splinter directly above Kevin's fingers. It was breaking! As it splintered, Kevin moved his fingers upward to force more of the door away from the wall. The fire crackled and flames were reaching for the front of the stall. Polly, completely terrified, pushed up against Kevin. "Get away from me!" he yelled. But Polly, too afraid to move closer to the flames, continued to push.

Kevin was now able to squeeze his whole body between the plywood and the wall. Forcing all of his bodyweight onto the plywood, he grunted as he gave one final push. The ancient nails gave way and the door splintered apart. As the door crumbled, Kevin lost his balance and fell to the floor.

Seeing a way out, Polly charged through the opening, stumbling over Kevin as she ran. The trainer screamed as the mare disappeared into the darkness.

Into The Night

As Polly dashed away from the barn, several embers from the fire fell onto her back. The ashes sizzled and burned the mare's hair just behind her withers. The instant sting, combined with her fear, made Polly run even faster.

The mare's escape was slowed by the heavy overgrowth in the small, abandoned turnouts. Years of neglect had allowed bushes and even a few small trees to take root near the barn. Thorn bushes with long, sharp barbs blocked her path, biting at the mare's sides. As Polly pushed her way through, the thorns ripped at her skin.

The old, wooden fence at the end of the run was not enough to stop the horse. She crashed through it, fell to her knees, and hit her head on the soft, muddy ground.

Pausing for only a second, Polly struggled to her feet. The mud from the morning's rain had made the ground slippery, but Polly refused to stop. She regained her footing and sped off into the night.

"Oh, my arm," groaned Kevin as he slowly pulled himself up off the ground. An agonizing pain shot up and down his left arm, and he knew instantly that it was broken. "If I ever get my hands on that horse," he told himself, "I'll . . ." the words drifted away. In horrible pain and unable to see beyond the overgrowth, the trainer knew he needed to concentrate on getting away from the fire. With light from the blaze showing him the way, he stumbled into the same thorn bushes through which Polly had crashed.

Kevin kept his left arm close to his chest while he used his right hand to push away the bushes. As he neared the broken fence, he heard the sound of sirens approaching. Realizing a neighbor must have called the fire department, he was relieved to know he would soon have assistance.

With his left arm useless, Kevin hurried as best he could towards the broken fence. He slowly climbed over the smashed boards while thorn bushes that had entwined themselves on the wood grabbed at him. But Kevin, too weary from the pain and fearful of the fire, ignored the thorns as they ripped his shirt. Stumbling onto the other side of the fence, the young trainer rushed away from the searing flames.

By the time Kevin reached the upper barn, two fire trucks had pulled into the yard. He leaned against the door of the building as the vehicles slowly made their way along the bumpy dirt driveway to the lower barn. As the trucks passed Kevin, two men jumped down and ran to Kevin's aid.

"Are you hurt?" asked one of the men.

"Yeah," replied Kevin, out of breath. "I think I broke my arm."

"Is anybody in that building?" asked the second firefighter.

"No. Nobody. I'm the only one here."

"What about animals? Are there horses in that barn?" Kevin looked over at the building, which was engulfed in flames. It was clear the structure would soon fall to the ground. There was no way to save it, and it would be impossible for anybody to go into it now.

"No, there . . ." Kevin stopped in mid-sentence. He suddenly realized this was his chance to get rid of the mare he hated so much. Polly had fled into the night. Who knew where she would end up? Hopefully she would run far away. "There was one horse," said Kevin cautiously, changing his story. "A show horse. But it's too late now . . ."

Polly charged through the woods behind the barn, diving around trees, ducking beneath low branches, and stumbling on tree roots as she ran. The glow from the fire lit her way briefly, but as she continued deeper into the forest, the light faded. With a cloudy sky covering the moon, it was difficult for the mare to see anything, but the lack of light had very little effect on the panicked horse. She never stopped to think about where she was headed; she simply ran as fast as she could.

As the tree trunks blended into the darkness, Polly tripped constantly. Her sides hurt from the hard bark that pulled at her flesh, while branches from the same trees slashed her face. It wasn't long before the Morgan began breathing heavily, and her neck lathered up with sweat. Polly's nostrils flared as she gasped for air. Forced to stop running, Polly slowed from a gallop to a canter and then to a trot.

Passing through a muddy area, Polly was startled as the ground suddenly fell out from beneath her. Level footing gave way to a steep hill, and as she tumbled forward, the mare unexpectedly splashed into a stream. Because the horse had spent her entire life as a show horse confined to a stall, she had never experienced the joy of playing in a stream. The water splashed up on her belly, while Polly, terrified at the strange new sensation, rushed across the stream. Quickly coming to the other side, she struggled to climb the embankment. When she reached the top, Polly turned to the left and followed the stream further away from the barn.

As time passed, the horrid smell of burning wood and hay disappeared and with it, much of Polly's fear. It was now easier to travel through the woods because the mare had stumbled upon an old, abandoned logging road. The horse didn't understand what had happened to her, but felt the need to keep moving. She trotted, then cantered, then walked, and after catching her breath, she broke into a trot again. Something kept her going. After stopping to grab a clump of grass, Polly lifted her head and sniffed the air. There was no smell of fire, but there was also no smell of horses. The Morgan wanted to find other horses, so she kept going down the road.

Shortly after midnight, the thick cloud cover began to break up, and by early morning, stars appeared in the sky. Polly continued to follow the road as it meandered up and down gentle hills, through deserted hayfields, into marshy, muddy sections and spots where the road had been washed away by many years of heavy rainstorms.

With the approach of dawn, the exhausted mare stopped to eat. She had found an especially lush area of green grass and gobbled down the tasty food. Her fear of the fire had subsided, although she still felt nervous because her instincts told her to be cautious. She swished her tail and kept stomping her front feet to chase away the many biting insects that were attracted to the horse by the smell of sweat.

Polly continued to graze until she heard a far off whinny. Raising her head up, ears forward, the mare patiently waited. Another whinny. Polly screamed in reply. Pausing for a moment, the mare then screamed again. This time the reply came immediately. Desperately longing for the companionship of other horses, Polly flew into a gallop and headed toward the sound.

Within a few strides, the mare reached the road she had been following the night before. The exhausted horse jumped over the old dirt road and ran into the woods, once again dodging fallen branches, tree stumps, and rocks. She continued to call to the other horse as she ran, each time hearing a response.

After several minutes, Polly stopped. She arched her neck, pricked her ears forward, and listened. No sound.

Frustrated, Polly called out. Her unknown friend again answered, but this time the response was loud and clear. She must be getting close. The Morgan broke into a canter and quickly came to an opening. Tall grass, up to her knees, surrounded her. Polly slowed to a trot, not sure if she should continue, but her instinct to be with other horses was too strong to ignore, so she proceeded up a small hill. From the top, the mare could see a white fence, and beyond that, several horses. Polly let out an ear-piercing call and galloped to the fence.

Five Arabian mares of various colors carefully watched the Morgan draw near. At first they hesitated, unsure of this new visitor. Was this horse a friend? Was it safe to approach? Always cautious, the Arabians slowly trotted forward, knees kicking up into the air as they gracefully floated through the pasture.

The herd leader, a gray mare with a mane that dropped down below her neck, led the way, with the other four horses obediently following her. The gray horse stopped about five feet from the fence, while Polly pushed against the rails, trying to get as close as possible. As Polly watched, the gray mare walked forward until their noses touched. Sniffing each other for a second, the gray let out a loud, threatening squeal and spun around so that her hind end faced Polly. Her back feet flew out to hit Polly, but the fence prevented the hooves from making contact with the Morgan's chest. Instead, the feet harmlessly hit the board.

The gray horse once again approached Polly. This time the Arabian leaned her head over the fence and ran her nose along Polly's shoulder. Not recognizing the strange, new smell, the Arabian flattened her ears, raised her tail, and once again turned her rump towards the fence. As the Arabian readied herself to kick, Polly backed up a step. The Morgan stretched out her head and snapped her lips together several times as a sign of submission.

The Arabian next trotted along the fence line and Polly followed. The other pastured horses came along too, curious to learn who the intruder was. As the horses strutted through the field, loudly talking to each other, the early morning mist began to disappear.

At the same time, a tall, thin man strolled out of a barn at the other end of the field. Hearing the commotion, he looked in the direction of his broodmare band and soon spotted the new arrival. "What the . . . ?" he asked himself. Returning to the barn, he grabbed a halter and lead rope and headed toward the horses. A few minutes later he arrived near the mares, his ugly, worn-out work boots soaked with morning dew. "Easy Lacy. Take it easy girl," he cooed to the lead gray mare. The horse looked at her owner but then returned her attention to Polly. The farmer walked over to the fence, bent down, and crawled between two of the rails. The Morgan eagerly came up to him and rubbed her sweaty chest and head on his stomach. "Hey, now, take it easy," he calmly told the Morgan. "Hungry, huh? Where did you come from?" he wondered as he carefully slipped the halter on the horse. Snapping the lead onto the halter, he walked the mare away as he told her, "Let's get you fed and then see if we can find your owner."

"Hey, Joe!" greeted the farmer into his phone. "It's Bill. Got a question for ya."

"What's up?" asked Joe. "Is everything okay?"

"Yeah, yeah, everything's fine."

"Are you sure?"

"Yeah, really. I'm fine," continued Bill. "I was wondering if you have any idea where a missing horse could be from?"

"What're you talking about?" asked Joe.

"Did you hear all the squealing this morning?" asked Bill.

"Yeah, I did. Figured ol'Lacy must have gotten out again and was driving one of the stallions crazy."

"Nope, that wasn't what was cause'n the ruckus."

"No?"

"Nope. I found a loose horse this morning running up and down my fence line. A mare, and she's all scratched up, like she was running through thorn bushes or something."

"A loose horse? Really?" asked Joe in disbelief.

"Yeah. Anyway," continued Bill, "I'm trying to figure out where the mare might be from. Any idea?"

"Nah, no idea. Hey, wait a minute. I heard there was a barn fire at Spencer's place in Carlton last night."

"Carlton? That's gotta be 20 miles from here. Ya think the mare could have come that far in one night?"

"I dunno," replied Joe. "That's pretty far to travel in the dark."

"You're right. But I'll give him a call, just in case. Oh, and if you hear of anybody looking for a missing horse, chestnut mare, let me know. Thanks."

Bill headed back out to his barn to check on the Morgan. The horse, who had been extremely nervous when she was first brought into the barn, had settled down and was quietly eating hay. Seeing the farmer, the horse nickered, walked around a tight circle, and then turned her attention back to her hay. All the other horses were out in the pastures, so the barn was very quiet. "Well, you can't stay here," said Bill as he approached the stall and studied the mare. *The horse is obviously a quality animal, probably a purebred, and somebody, somewhere, must be missing her*, thought Bill. "I don't have enough room in my barn as it is, and I sure as heck don't need another horse, especially one who isn't an Arabian," he told the horse. His plans only included raising registered Arabians, so he couldn't afford to keep a horse of unknown breeding simply as a pet. Tossing another flake of hay to the mare, the farmer headed outside to check on his horses.

That evening, Bill called Spencer's Training Barn, but there was no answer. In fact, for the next three days, every time he called, he got an answering machine. He left several messages and was disappointed that nobody returned his calls. Bill was sure the horse was from Spencer's because he couldn't find anybody else who was missing a horse. He called Animal Control, the local police, and numerous boarding and training barns in the area but each time the answer was the same; "Nope, not us."

Finally, on the fourth day, when Bill called Spencer's Training Barn, a man answered. "Yeah, what do you want?" asked the rude voice.

"My name is Bill Johnson. I own the Arabian farm over in Chesterfield. Four days ago, a chestnut mare wandered onto my property. She looks like a Morgan. I'm trying to find her owner. I heard you had a fire and thought maybe she'd escaped."

"No, not us," growled Mr. Spencer. "Our lower barn burned to the ground, but my assistant trainer was the only one who got out alive. The horse who lived in the barn didn't survive. Thanks, anyway." The phone line clicked as Mr. Spencer hung up without even saying goodbye.

After the fire, Kevin had told Mr. Spencer that Polly had been in the barn and was too afraid to come out with him. When he was asked how he had broken his arm, Kevin lied to his boss and said that the obnoxious horse had rammed her whole body into him as she ran around her stall. But still the horse had refused to leave the stall. Mr. Spencer saw no reason to doubt his assistant and he was glad the mare was gone.

Meanwhile, Bill Johnson was stuck with a mysterious horse who nobody seemed to want. He certainly couldn't afford to keep the mare, so he decided, after making all attempts to find her owner, to sell her at the local auction.

Polly was brought to the auction the next week and purchased by a fast-talking horse trader. During the next few years, the beautiful Morgan mare would have several owners. Although she never found herself in the hands of a person as uncaring as Jim Spencer or his assistant Kevin, she also never belonged to anybody who truly loved her.

Buying Another Morgan?

"What do you want to do?"

"I dunno. What do you want to do?"

Heather thought for a minute. The avid rider was anxious to work her stallion, but she'd spent the last hour cleaning stalls, sweeping the barn aisle and tack room, and bringing hay down from the loft for the evening feeding. Now her toes were frozen and she could hardly feel her fingers. It was early February and it was cold outside! "Let's go ask Mrs. Campbell for something hot to drink. We can warm up and then come back out for a short ride," she finally suggested.

"Okay, sounds good," happily agreed Karen.

Heather and Karen made their way up to the house. They both boarded their horses at Gallant Morgan Horse Farm and had become good friends. Karen owned Robin, a very sweet and somewhat lazy bay Morgan mare. The horse was a perfect match for the fourteen-year-old, a shy person who was learning to be confident around a barn full of horses. Karen was also the proud owner of Rerun, a spunky gray and white Miniature Horse. Rerun was too small to ride but she was a fabulous driving horse with an amazingly fast road trot. Heather, a sixteen-year-old, had a natural talent for riding even the most difficult horses. She owned the gorgeous black Morgan stallion Blackjack, as well as a rare gray Morgan mare, Frosty, and her daughter, Shadow. She also loved to ride Rusty, a bay Morgan gelding who belonged to Chauncy Campbell, the owner of the farm. Rusty loved to jump and had taught Heather how to fly over the highest obstacles.

The barn had ten stalls and at one time had been full of Morgan Horses, from babies to old broodmares. But after Chauncy had become ill, most of the horses were sold. Now Chauncy was healthy and the barn was slowly filling up again, thanks to Heather and Karen.

"Hi, Mrs. Campbell!" exclaimed Heather as she and Karen entered the Campbells' house.

"Oh, Heather, hi," replied Mrs. Campbell as she came down the hallway toward the kitchen. At her side, barking in a frenzy of happiness, was Champ, Heather's rambunctious dachshund. He came to the farm almost every day with Heather, but during the cold weather, spent his time in the Campbells' house. "I'll bet you girls are frozen. Would you like something hot to drink?"

Both girls smiled. As they took off their gloves and boots, they continued to discuss their plans for the day. "We could work the horses in the ring," suggested Karen.

"It looked a little icy out there," said Heather. "How about a trail ride? The snowmobiles packed the snow down pretty well."

"Sure!" agreed Karen. "As soon as I warm up!"

"Here you go, Karen," said Mrs. Campbell as she handed the girl a steaming mug of hot chocolate with plenty of whipped cream decorating the top.

"Thank you!"

"Oh, thank you so much," added Heather as Mrs. Campbell handed her a mug too. Heather slurped the whipped cream and then slowly sipped the hot chocolate, careful not to burn her tongue. "Mmm, it's so good," she said as the heat slowly made its way from her lips to her stomach. Heather knew that Mrs. Campbell delighted in knowing her snacks were enjoyed, and Heather never failed to show her appreciation.

"Chauncy? Where are you? Are you ready for some hot chocolate?" Mrs. Campbell called out.

"I'll be there in a minute," came a voice from the other end of the house.

Heather and Karen settled in at the kitchen table with the mugs of hot chocolate. Champ immediately jumped into his owner's lap, curled into a ball, and fell asleep.

Heather and Karen began to discuss the upcoming show season. It was one of their favorite topics.

"Are you going to show Blackjack?" asked Karen.

"Oh, yeah!" replied Heather. "He's so much fun to show. Maybe I can show Rusty in a couple of jumping shows, and it'd be a blast to take Frosty on an overnight trail ride too. What about Robin? Do you think you'd like to show her?"

"Maybe," answered Karen. She had shown Robin once and had loved the experience. "If we practice a lot, I think—"

"Are you ladies talking about showing again?" interrupted Chauncy. He knew Heather loved to show and was doing her best to get Karen involved too. "Well, there's nothing wrong with that," decided Chauncy. "It helps pass the long winter days. Oh, that reminds me. Heather?"

"Yes?"

"I've been meaning to ask you," Chauncy paused, then continued, "I'd like to enter Blackjack in the Justin Morgan class at the Vermont Country Show this spring."

"Justin Morgan class?" asked Karen. "What's that?"

"Oh, I've heard of that class," enthused Heather. "That's where the horses have to race, then show in the ring, and then pull a heavy weight, right?"

"Pretty much," said Chauncy. "First, they race a half a mile in harness, at the trot, then they race under saddle at a full-out gallop, then they're shown in a pleasure class and finally, each horse has to pull a 500-pound stone boat 20 feet."

"Stone boat?" asked Heather. "What's that?"

"Basically it's a flat board with 500 pounds of cement blocks on it."

"And the whole thing is done one event after the other, with no real time in between to rest?"

"Yup," said Chauncy, "just like Justin Morgan used to do."

"Cool!" whispered Karen.

"Do you think Blackjack can do it, Chauncy?" asked Heather.

"Yes, I think he'd actually do really well. He already rides and drives and has a great road trot, and we know he loves to show. I'd have to get him used to the work harness and pulling a weight, but I've got plenty of time for that. And you would have to work him up and down the road, getting him to stretch out that road trot and racing the other horses. That would help strengthen him and increase his speed in harness. Probably get him going against Frosty. She has the fastest road trot."

"What about having Blackjack practice with Robin? She can trot," suggested Karen.

Chauncy knew that Karen adored Robin, but he also knew the mare was rather slow and Blackjack would quickly leave her in the dust. "You could certainly try. I'm sure it'd be fun, but I think Blackjack might need a faster competitor."

"It sounds really neat," said Heather. "Would I get to ride Blackjack?"

"Of course," said Chauncy. "You'd ride him in the galloping race and show him in the ring class, and I'd drive him in the trotting race and get him to pull the stone boat."

"He's not super fast at the gallop," noted Heather. "I don't know how well we'd do in that part."

"It'd probably be his weakest event, but since he's so good at everything else, I think he'd be fine."

"Yeah, let's do it!" Heather squealed.

"Great! As soon as the weather gets a little better, I'll drag the stone boat out from the shed and start practicing," said Chauncy, with as much enthusiasm as Heather. "You should start working him at the road trot, but be careful, not too much yet. And no galloping until spring when the ice and mud are gone. I think—" as Chauncy continued, the phone rang.

"Chauncy, it's for you. It's Mike," said Mrs. Campbell as she handed her husband the phone receiver.

"Hi Mike. What's up?"

As Chauncy talked, Karen and Heather began to make plans for getting Blackjack ready for the Justin Morgan class. They ignored Chauncy's conversation until they heard, "a horse? No, I don't need another one, why do you ask?"

Heather and Karen turned and looked at Chauncy. Heather's eyebrows went up and she leaned towards Chauncy, trying to figure out what horse the caller was talking about. "Okay, sure,

Mike. No, I don't but I'll come look at her anyway. I'll be there tomorrow afternoon at two."

"What horse?" asked Heather, as Chauncy hung up the phone.

"My friend Mike was given a horse recently that he can't keep. He thinks it's a Morgan, so he thought of me. I'm going to look at her tomorrow. Would you ladies like to come?"

Both girls smiled.

Gray clouds gradually overtook the crisp, clear sunshine of the early morning. As Heather and Karen left the barn for home, snowflakes began to slowly fall from the sky. By dusk, the snow was falling at a blinding pace and around midnight the wind picked up, creating enormous snowdrifts.

When Heather woke up the following morning, she peered out her window and could barely see ten feet beyond her house. What a good morning to sleep late! The sleepy girl returned to her bed and crawled under her blankets. Lying under her thick, warm comforter, she listened as the wind pounded at her window. Heather gradually fell back to sleep but was awakened an hour later as a snowplow rumbled down the street.

Heather stretched, yawned, and got out of bed. This time, when she looked out the window, she was greeted with glaring sunshine. "Wow, it's so bright out," she mumbled as she headed to the kitchen to make a phone call. "Hi, this is Heather. Is Chauncy there?"

When Chauncy came to the phone, Heather asked him if the trip to visit the horse was cancelled.

"No, I'm still going," he replied. "It isn't very far from here and I'm not planning on going until after lunch. The roads should be clear by then. Do you still want to come?"

"Of course," said Heather. "I just have to make sure my dad will take me. I'll call you if I can't come. Otherwise, I'll be there right after lunch."

The trip to Chauncy's farm was slow and a bit slippery. Mr. Richardson, who loved to drive in all sorts of weather, had volunteered to take Chauncy, Karen, and Heather to visit the horse. When they arrived at Chauncy's, Karen was already there, out in the barn playing with Robin. Within minutes, she and Chauncy were packed into Mr. Richardson's car and the group was headed to Kingston Quarter Horses, the temporary home of the mysterious horse.

"Hey, Mike! How are you?" asked Chauncy as he climbed out of the car.

Mike Kimball was out in his yard, shoveling snow from the sidewalk in front of his house. He happily tossed the shovel aside when he saw his old friend. "Chauncy! It's good to see you. Thanks so much for coming. I have to admit that I'm at a bit of a loss; I don't know what to do with the mare I called about. She's real nice, got a good temperament, really solid conformation, and I'm pretty sure she's a Morgan. Unfortunately, I can't keep her. I don't have any room right now, in fact, I don't even have a stall for her."

"Where'd she come from?" asked Chauncy.

"I got her from a gal about 30 miles from here, over in Attleboro. Her daughter had ridden the mare last fall, but when the weather turned cold, the girl lost interest. Since then, the horse has been sitting around in a stall. The mother was tired of feeding the horse and cleaning the stall. Said she didn't want the horse to go to waste. Honestly, Chauncy, she gave me the horse for free and I thought I'd be able to sell her quickly, but I don't have the time to market her, and she's getting picked on by my other mares, so I need to find her a home right away. I'd be happy to give her to you; I don't need to get anything for her. I'd just like to cut my losses and not spend any more money feeding her. I thought maybe you could use her in your breeding program."

"Does she have papers?" asked Chauncy, who knew if the horse didn't have registration papers, her foals would be much less valuable. It didn't make any sense for Chauncy to breed grade horses. If the foals couldn't be registered, he didn't want the mare.

"She doesn't," admitted Mike. "But maybe you could get them," he suggested, hoping Chauncy would take a chance on the horse. "I could give you the name and phone number of the woman who gave her to me. Maybe she could give you the name of the previous owner and you could get papers from them. I'm sure this mare is a purebred; she's way too nice to be a grade horse."

"Well, we might as well take a look at her," said Chauncy, making up his mind that he wouldn't take the horse.

Mr. Kimball led the way past his house to a big pasture. The path to the pasture had not yet been plowed and the snow was knee-deep. Heather found herself picking her feet up, much like a high-stepping show horse, to keep the snow from getting over the tops of her boots. "Sorry about all the snow," apologized Mr. Kimball. He stopped at a fence, squeezed between the boards, and motioned the others to follow. "She's in here."

Heather looked out into the pasture, her eyes blinking from the glare of the bright sun bouncing off the freshly fallen snow. She saw two big run-in sheds with several horses standing nearby, eating hay. Off in a corner stood one lonely horse, her head hanging down low, with several long, thin icicles hanging off her mane. *The mare*, thought Heather, *seems to be in good shape*. As they approached, Heather noticed the horse also had numerous icicles hanging from her forelock and body. She even had tiny little icicles on her eyelashes. But under all that ice and winter hair, Heather saw a beautiful Morgan Horse. She looked dark chestnut and had a large white star smack in the middle of her forehead and a small snip of white on the tip of her nose. She had tiny little ears and big, expressive eyes like those of Blackjack, her favorite horse.

"The other horses don't seem to like the newcomer and won't let her into the shed. With the storm coming yesterday, I knew it would be tough on her," explained Mr. Kimball, perhaps feeling a bit guilty about the mare's condition. "But I don't have an extra stall and this was the only place I could put her."

"She was outside during the storm last night?" asked Karen.

"Unfortunately, yes. A lot of times my horses will be out in the worst weather, rain, sleet, freezing rain, and they seem perfectly happy. I sometimes think they prefer the foul weather to standing in their sheds. It's the wind that bothers them though. When the wind starts to blow, you'll see all these horses clamor to get inside their shelters. But my other horses won't let the new horse in either of the sheds, even in the bad weather. So, I really need to find her a home," concluded Mr. Kimball. "What do you think, Chauncy?"

Chauncy was already investigating the mare, carefully looking her over from top to bottom. The mare had perked up when she realized she had visitors, and she carefully watched them to see what they wanted. "She sure looks like a Morgan," said Chauncy, speaking to no one in particular. Looking in her mouth, he continued, "My guess is that she's about seven years old; maybe eight." He then picked up one of her front feet, tapping the hoof and then putting the leg down again. Taking his gloves off, he ran his hands down all four legs, checking for problems. "She's got good legs," he mumbled.

Meanwhile, Heather caught the mare's attention. The friendly horse sniffed one of Heather's jacket pockets, her nose trying to wiggle its way inside. "I don't have anything for you," said Heather as she stroked the mare's neck. Looking at all the icicles, Heather began to gently pull them off the mare's hide, one at a time. "Poor thing," she cooed, "you need a home, don't you? And somebody to love and spoil you too."

"Heather," warned Mr. Richardson. "Don't you go getting any crazy ideas. We're not in the market for another horse. Three horses is plenty."

"But I only have two," whined Karen, in a playful voice. She knew her parents would never allow her to get another horse, and she was happy to only have Robin and Rerun to take care of every day.

As the group continued to look at the mare, the other horses grew jealous and wandered over to get some attention. The herd leader, a chestnut mare with a wide white blaze covering much of her head, flattened her ears and trotted toward the new horse.

*"Poor thing," she cooed, "you need
a home, don't you?"*

The ice-covered mare squealed in panic and pushed her way through the visitors and trotted away. "Look at her go!" marveled Heather. "That sure looks like a Morgan trot!" The mare flew across the snow, her legs bouncing up high above the white powder. With ears pricked forward and head held high, she oozed Morgan.

"Free, huh?" asked Chauncy.

"Yes. I just need you to take her soon," answered Mr. Kimball.

"She sure would make a nice addition to my barn. You said the woman you got her from was riding her? So she's broke to ride?"

"The daughter was riding her. But I can't speak for how well she's trained."

"Well, if I can track down her papers, then I could breed her and get my breeding program started up again. I sure do miss having foals around the barn. Free, huh?"

Mr. Kimball laughed. "Yes, Chauncy. Free. If you can't get her papers, then you can probably sell her in the spring for a decent profit. What's the risk?"

Chauncy studied the mare carefully and smiled. Heather looked at Karen and the two girls smiled too. They knew that there would soon be a new horse at Gallant Morgan Horse Farm.

WHO IS SHE?

"**I**s she here? Is she here yet?" squealed Heather as she jumped off the school bus. The eager girl didn't bother to see if Chauncy was up at the house; she dashed off to the barn so she could meet the new Morgan right away.

"Slow down," advised Chauncy as he peered out through the open barn door. "You might think you've never seen a horse before!"

"Is she here?" asked Heather again, trying to catch her breath after her quick run.

"Yes, she's here. She's in the first stall on the right."

Looking inside the stall, Heather saw a very fuzzy, dark chestnut mare with a long, knotted mane and tail. The icicles that had hung from her hide when Heather last saw her were gone, but otherwise, she looked the same. The horse was eating some hay Chauncy had given her earlier. "She looks like she could use some love," murmured Heather as she entered the stall. "Hey, there, um, horse? Oh, Chauncy?"

"Yeah?"

"What's her name?"

"I haven't decided yet. You'll have to help me come up with a good name."

"What do you want to be called?" asked Heather as she turned her attention back to the horse. The mare walked over to Heather and softly nuzzled her jacket. Reaching out with her gloved hand, Heather stroked the mare's neck. "Let's see, what would be a good name?" The mare, still standing next to the girl, decided to rub her head hard against the soft winter jacket. "Whoa! Cut that out," scolded Heather as she almost tumbled over from the force of the horse's heavy head on her chest. "We could call you Itchy but that's a silly name. How about Sweetie? No, that's dumb. Um, Brownie?"

"Brownie?" asked Chauncy in disbelief. "You want to name my horse after a snack?"

"No, Chauncy. She's a brown horse. If Nicholas can name his Appaloosa Spot, then why can't we name a horse Brownie?"

"Because I don't want people to laugh at my horse's name. Besides, she's not brown, she's chestnut."

"Well, she looks brown."

"Why don't we wait to name her until we know her personality a little better? Something will come up."

"Sure, Chauncy. You're right. We'll think of a good name for her, don't worry. Oh, Chauncy? Can't you ask the lady who owned her before Mr. Kimball what her name is?"

"Yup, and I plan to do just that. Mike gave me her phone number, but I haven't been able to reach her yet. As soon as I do, I'll find out what they called her. And hopefully we'll be able to track down her original owner too. Remember, don't get too attached to Brownie," smiled Chauncy. "If I can't get her papers, then I can't afford to keep her. Unregistered grade horses are not worth much money. And their foals are worth even less. I'd spend more money feeding any foal than I'd ever recoup on its sale price."

"I know, Chauncy. I won't get attached," agreed Heather. But as the words came out, the friendly mare lifted her head to Heather's face and blew the girl a warm kiss. She could feel herself falling in love already.

Later that week, after the new arrival had had a chance to settle into her new home, Heather took her out to the ring to be worked for the first time. She had lunged the mare several times, and the horse seemed to be calm and obedient. Not knowing how the horse had been trained, Heather used a hunt saddle and a gentle snaffle bit in the mare's mouth.

As Heather gathered her reins to mount, the horse shook her head and pawed the ground. "Anxious to get going?" asked the girl as she slipped into the saddle. The horse took a step forward but stopped when Heather pulled back slightly on the reins. "Not yet, girl. Be patient. Let me get into the saddle first." Heather quickly adjusted her position and then asked the mare to move forward. But instead, the horse turned her head towards Heather and nuzzled her foot. "What are you doing, silly girl?" Stroking the mare's neck with one hand, she continued, "You're a goofy horse, you know that? Do you realize that, Annie Bananie?" No sooner were the words out of Heather's mouth than she realized she had found the horse's new name—Annie. "Hey, Chauncy?" she called to the old man approaching the ring.

"Yes?" he answered.

"I just named your new horse."

"Uh, oh. I'm afraid to ask."

"No, it's a good name, really. Her name is Annie. As in Annie Bananie."

"Annie Bananie?"

"Yes! Isn't it a cute name?" asked Heather.

Chauncy thought for a moment as he leaned on the fence. "Well, it's certainly better than Brownie. Okay, we'll call her Annie until we find out her real name. Now let's see what she can do."

Heather rode the mare to the rail and put her through her paces. The horse knew how to walk, trot, and canter, but she didn't seem very happy about it. "Try to relax your body," instructed Chauncy as he slipped through the gate and walked into the center of the ring. "She's awful uptight. See how she's tossing her head?"

"But my reins aren't that tight," replied Heather as she slowed Annie down to a walk. The mare, who had been trotting, obeyed her rider, but, as Chauncy noted, also threw her head up high.

"It's not your hands, Heather. Some previous owner must have been pretty rough on her. I'll also get the dentist out here next week to check her teeth. Maybe she's got a tooth with a sharp edge that's cutting into her cheek."

"Easy, Annie. Good girl, that's it," soothed Heather. The new horse didn't want to do a flat-footed walk. Instead she jigged, bouncing her rider around in the saddle. "She feels tense, Chauncy."

"I can see it. You'll have to show her that you're not going to hurt her."

"She's not doing anything bad, though," continued Heather. "She just doesn't seem happy."

"She also looks more like a saddle seat horse, with that high neck-set and all her leg action."

"Oh, good!" enthusiastically replied Heather. "Another saddle seat horse. Watch out, Blackjack!"

"Who are you riding?" asked a voice from near the barn. Heather looked up and saw Nicholas Bunker, one of her best friends. Nicholas was mounted on Spot, his constant riding companion and one of the best jumping horses Heather had ever seen. Nicholas lived nearby and often rode his horse to Chauncy's place to visit and ride with Heather.

"This is Annie," Heather replied as she dismounted and led Chauncy's horse to the barn.

"You bought a new horse?" asked Nicholas in disbelief. "What's Blackjack going to say?"

"Blackjack likes her," answered Heather. "He whinnies to her a lot." Thinking for a moment, Heather added, "It's almost as if he knows her."

"But another horse?" complained Nicholas.

"I didn't buy another horse. She's not mine. She belongs to Chauncy. I'm just exercising her."

"She's cute! What are you going to do with her, Chauncy?"

"Annie is Chauncy's new broodmare," blurted out Heather before Chauncy had a chance to reply.

"Really? That's great. More foals running around Gallant Morgans."

"Only if we can get her registration papers," interrupted Chauncy. Chauncy explained the situation to Nicholas while Heather put Annie back into her stall and got Blackjack ready for riding.

"All set?" asked Heather as she mounted Blackjack.

"Yup," replied Nicholas. "Where do you want to go?"

"Can we go down the road? I need to start working on Blackjack's road trot."

"Why?" asked Nicholas.

Heather then told her friend all about their plans to show Blackjack in the Justin Morgan class at the Vermont show in June. "I need to practice with another horse so he'll get used to racing. It will also teach him to go faster and faster at the road trot."

Blackjack, Spot, and their riders headed down Mill Creek Road. The old, bumpy road had very little traffic and within half a mile turned to dirt. It was also straight and flat, a perfect place to work on Blackjack's trot.

As the group approached the area where the pavement ended, Heather gathered up her reins, turned to Nicholas, and asked, "Are you ready?"

"For what?" he replied.

"Road trot!" hollered Heather as she urged Blackjack into action.

"Hey! That's cheating," protested Nicholas as he asked Spot to move out. The Appaloosa quickly came to life and broke into a trot. The bold, black Morgan stallion was already several feet ahead of them and gaining ground fast. The road, which had been plowed, was nonetheless covered in mud from the melting snow. The slush flew up into Spot's face, and he threw his head as a blob of mud hit him on the nose. "That's not fair!" yelled Nicholas to his opponent. "We don't have a chance to catch you."

Heather and Blackjack were now far in front of their competitors. The girl smiled and turned to look at her friend, now partially covered in mud like his horse. Heather's boots and Blackjack's belly were spattered with brown gunk, but nothing like Spot and Nicholas. She slowed her horse to a walk and waited for Nicholas to catch up. "I think I need to give you a head start," she laughed.

Nicholas took off his blue wire-rimmed glasses and wiped a splotch of muck off one lens. Slipping the glasses back on, he gave Heather an evil glance and, without a word, urged his horse back into a trot.

"No fair!" yelled Heather as she asked Blackjack for another road trot. The Morgan hated to be behind any other horse and eagerly took up the chase. His ears were flat against his neck, showing his displeasure with being last. Within several strides, he was neck and neck with Spot. Heather glared at Nicholas and asked, "Ready to eat some more mud?" In a competitive tone she told her horse, "Come on boy, let's show them who's the boss!"

Try as he might, Spot was no match for the Morgan. The Appaloosa's talent lay in soaring over big jumps, not in trotting down a muddy road.

In contrast, Blackjack had generations of trotting horses in his blood. He had a huge, ground-covering trot and naturally moved out in a fast, high-stepping gait.

The moment Blackjack passed Spot, the stallion's ears shot forward. As long as he was out in front, the competitive Morgan was happy. Passing the Appaloosa, Blackjack didn't slow down. In fact, it seemed to Heather that her horse was increasing his speed.

In less than a minute, Blackjack and Heather were well beyond Spot and Nicholas. The girl looked over her shoulder and saw Nicholas trying his best to urge his horse into a faster trot, but there was nothing the talented rider could do to get any more speed from his mount.

"I think we won!" announced Heather as she slowed Blackjack to a walk. Her horse was breathing hard, and as Spot approached, it was easy to see that he too, was a bit tired. "They're sorta out of shape so we should probably take it easy. Besides, I don't want Blackjack to break a sweat; with his thick winter coat I'll never get him cooled down." Heather knew that once a horse started sweating in the winter, it took a long time for the animal to dry off. It also made it easy for the horse to catch a chill. "Let's walk them home."

The following day, while Heather was tacking Annie up for a ride, Chauncy came into the barn. "I have some news," he told his friend.

"You heard from Annie's last owner?" asked Heather in anticipation.

"Yes, she finally called."

"And?"

"And her name is Cookie."

"Cookie? Ew, that's a horrible name!"

"I agree. It might be a good name for a short, fat pony, but not an elegant, showy Morgan mare."

"Do I have to call her Cookie?" asked a disappointed Heather.

"I don't see why we need to call her that. Let's keep her name Annie, at least until we find out her real name."

"Cookie's not her real name? I'm confused," stated Heather, trying to figure out what Chauncy was talking about.

"Oh, I'm sorry, I didn't explain. Mrs. Patrick, the woman who owned Cookie, I mean Annie, isn't the horse's original owner. She purchased the mare from a woman in Milford, so now I've got to track that woman down."

"Did Mrs. Patrick give you a phone number for the other lady?" asked Heather.

"No, she didn't have one; she threw away all the information she had on the horse after she bought the mare. But I have a name, a Mrs. Collins. I tried calling but the number is unlisted. I called Mrs. Patrick back and she thought she remembered the street that Mrs. Collins lives on. So I've written a letter and will hopefully hear back. If I can't get Annie's registration papers soon, I may have to sell her . . ." He didn't like the thought of selling the pretty mare, as he too, was getting attached to the friendly horse. Changing the subject, he asked, "I see you're going to ride her today. Saddle seat too? Good. I think that will be a better match for her."

Heather finished tacking up Annie and then rode her under Chauncy's watchful eye. She didn't use a fancy full bridle with its two bits and double reins as required in the show ring. Instead she used a training bridle with a single bit and set of reins, but she rode in the traditional flat saddle and positioned her body more upright as required by her change of riding style. Maybe Annie would like it better.

Heather's lesson progressed smoothly. Annie continued to obediently follow her rider's cues, although she still wouldn't walk. The horse, who had been trained by Jim Spencer and his assistant Kevin, had learned through pain that she couldn't relax. She needed to be ready for anything and that meant jigging rather than walking. The bouncy, prancing gait jostled Heather around in the saddle a bit, but she was a good rider and knew how to handle a nervous horse.

Annie also kept her head higher than that of Rusty, Heather's jumping horse. When Annie had been ridden western by Kevin Jones, her mouth had been pulled hard, and strange contraptions had been attached to her face in an attempt to get her head down. Now, for the first time, she was being encouraged to carry her head in its natural position where it felt comfortable. The high head-set was a good match for a fancy saddle seat horse.

Walking along, Annie also threw her nose out over and over, as if she were trying to escape from the bit. In the past, the horse had been punished for this action, but Heather let her hands get pulled slightly forward by the horse. The girl didn't want the horse to fight; she wanted the horse to calm down.

Instead of punishing her horse, Heather relaxed her body and talked softly, trying to reassure the mare that nobody would hurt her. "She reminds me of Frosty when I first started to ride her," Heather told Chauncy. If only she'd known that Annie had been trained by the same heartless man as Frosty she would have understood what was wrong.

"I see the similarities, too," noted Chauncy. "But, unlike Frosty, I think you'll be able to get Annie to work well in the ring. Frosty was a lot more nervous. Annie is anxious, but she's listening, not fighting. It'll just take her a little while to quiet down."

Heather continued working the horse, spending far more time on the walk than the trot or canter.

It was best, Chauncy explained, to work on calming the mare first, so Heather walked a lot, then did a brief trot, then finally more walking. Eventually, Annie relaxed slightly and she was rewarded by ending her lesson. "Always finish on a positive note," Chauncy had repeatedly told Heather with each horse she had trained. Heather knew that rule very well.

While Heather cooled out the chestnut mare, Chauncy headed back to the barn. After about ten minutes, as Heather dismounted, Nicholas and Spot appeared. "Riding the new mare again?" he asked.

"Yeah. She's doing pretty well. Maybe by spring I'll be able to show her."

"At the spring Morgan show?" asked Nicholas.

"No, I can't, not unless we get her papers by then. I'll probably take her to a small open show. So, are you ready to race Blackjack again?"

"I dunno," replied Nicholas. "I think Spot's feelings were hurt yesterday."

Heather giggled. "Blackjack is pretty fast at the trot, isn't he? Hey! I know what we should do. Why don't you ride Frosty? She's got an awesome road trot and will give Blackjack a run for the money."

Nicholas quickly agreed to the challenge. He led Spot to the ring, removed the saddle and bridle from the tall Appaloosa, and turned the horse loose in the ring. Next he headed into the barn to tack up Frosty.

It wasn't long before the two riders and their horses were headed down Mill Creek Road.

As they walked along, warming up the horses before they hit the dirt section, Heather gave Nicholas hints to riding Frosty. "She's not hard to ride," explained the girl, "just don't pull on her mouth. She hates that. Oh, and don't use too much leg on her or you'll never stop her. Other than that, she's easy."

"Gotcha," replied Nicholas, confident that he could handle the pretty gray Morgan.

"Let's not go full speed the first time," suggested Heather as she urged Blackjack into a trot. "Get a feel for Frosty first and then we'll let 'um loose."

Nicholas clucked to Frosty who instantly picked up the trot. Her springy, ground-covering gait was very different from Spot's slower trot, and it threw him off balance. As Nicholas pulled on the reins a little to regain his balance, Frosty threw her head up and took off. "Yikes! She's fast," he blurted out as he posted to the quick moving gait. Blackjack, refusing to be left behind, flattened his ears and quickened his pace. But this competitor was different from the one he flew past yesterday. Frosty was fast and she didn't want to let the black stallion win the race.

"So much for going slow!" yelled Heather as she and Blackjack caught up to Nicholas and Frosty. Seeing the stallion catching up, Frosty too flattened her ears against her neck. Nicholas had never experienced such a fast trot and had trouble posting to its quick movement. But he loved the thrill of the wind whipping past his face.

It took several paces before Blackjack was able to get ahead of the gray mare, but he didn't get very far. With his head stretched out, Blackjack's shoulder was next to Frosty's nose. "Look at their ears!" laughed Heather as she glided along on the back of her horse. Blackjack's ears shot forward the instant he passed Frosty. But then Frosty surged onward and as she briefly passed Blackjack, her ears flew forward while the stallion's shot back. The two horses took turns in the lead, the one in front with forward ears and the one falling to second, flattening its ears against its neck.

After several minutes, the riders asked their horses to walk. Neither horse wanted to walk and it took a bit of convincing, but with lots of "whoas" and gentle tugs at the reins, the horses finally slowed down. "Gosh, they don't like to lose, do they?" asked Nicholas.

"That's good!" replied Heather as they walked along. "It means that Blackjack will want to win those races in the Justin Morgan class."

"Maybe you should enter Frosty too," suggested Nicholas. "She's pretty fast!"

"Nah, we can't. Even though she's incredibly fast at the road trot, she doesn't drive and she hates ring work. Plus, I don't even know if she could pull a stone boat."

"A what?"

Heather explained the entire class to Nicholas.

"That's so neat," said Nicholas. "You know I want to come and watch."

"Of course," agreed Heather. "I'm sure Chauncy would love all the help he can get. I'm going to ride in the saddle race and show Blackjack in the ring class, and Chauncy is going to drive him in the harness race and do the stone boat pull."

"Sounds like a lot of fun."

"Yeah, but also really hard," said Heather. "So we better keep practicing. Ready?"

In a flash, the two horses dashed off again.

THE WILD BUGGY RIDE

The March mud was everywhere, but there was also a hint of spring in the air. The horses had started shedding their heavy winter coats and were eager to roll in the mucky, slushy mess in the center of Chauncy's ring.

Every time Heather put the horses out to play, they'd stroll to the middle, paw, circle, drop to their knees, and finally, plop down into the mud. Without exception, the horses would lie flat, rubbing the mud all over their bodies. Then they'd roll over to the other side, their legs flopping in the air as they turned. Frosty would only roll once, as would Shadow, Robin, and Rerun, but Rusty and Blackjack loved to roll over and over, as many as six or seven times. Once the mud was sufficiently plastered on the horse's body, the animal would slowly get up, lower its head, and shake violently. Then it almost always kicked up its heels, squealed, and ran off to play. They never tired of the routine, but Heather was definitely weary of cleaning them.

Arriving after school one day, Heather was disappointed to find all the horses soaked in mud. Blackjack, still out in the ring, was the wettest of all, and none were dry enough to ride. "I'll have to wait to ride," she sighed as she wandered over to the tack area and grabbed a pitchfork. "Guess I'll clean stalls today."

Quickly checking each stall to see which one needed the most cleaning, Heather was not surprised to see that Rusty's was a mess. "You're a big slob, aren't you?" she asked her favorite jumping horse as she entered the stall with the wheelbarrow. Getting to work, she was soon lost in thought and didn't hear Karen enter the barn. "Hey there," called Karen as she leaned over Rusty's stall door.

"Oh, hi Karen," replied Heather, a bit startled. "What's up?"

"Not much. I think I'm going to ride Robin today."

Smiling, Heather cautioned, "You might want to take a look at her first. She's covered in mud."

"Again?" sighed Karen. "You think she'd get tired of being so dirty."

"Nah," said Heather. "She loves the brushing once she's dried off. Besides, all that dirt flying around as you brush her is so much fun."

Karen rolled her eyes. "Oh, yeah," she replied sarcastically, "I love getting all that dirt on my jacket, on my face, and in my mouth. Bleck." Wandering over to Rerun's stall, Karen was excited to see that her Miniature Horse wasn't very dirty. "Looks like Rerun avoided the mud today. Maybe I'll lunge her." Walking the animal out of her stall, Karen brought Rerun to the front and attached the mare's halter to the cross ties. With so little horse to clean, it didn't take the girl long to groom her mare. Leading Rerun out to the front yard, Karen began working the playful horse. Blackjack, meanwhile, trotted over to the rail so he could get a good view. He whinnied softly to Rerun, but the horse ignored the stallion, as she was busy listening to her owner.

While Karen played with Rerun, Heather finished cleaning Rusty's stall and started on Blackjack's. The stallion was much neater than his stablemate, and soon Heather had removed the manure and dumped a load of fresh bedding in the stall. Pushing the wheelbarrow out of the stall, she saw Karen and Rerun returning from their workout. "Done already?" she asked.

"Yeah," replied Karen. "There's not a lot you can do with a horse running around in a circle."

Heather smiled. She knew there was actually quite a bit you could do, such as working on voice commands, body language, and various exercises, but she didn't want to disagree with Karen, a girl who always got bored quickly. Instead, she asked, "How was Rerun today?"

"She was fine," replied Karen. "Although a little frisky."

"Rerun is probably playful because spring is coming."

"Maybe," answered Karen, not really believing that Rerun was naughty because the weather was nice.

"Hey, I've got an idea," suggested Heather. "How about taking Rerun out for a drive? I'm guessing Chauncy will want to show her again this year, so it'd probably be a good idea to start working her in harness."

"Sure, go ahead," said Karen. "But I think I'll pass. I'd rather spend some time brushing Robin."

"Are you sure?" asked Heather. "It'll be fun, I promise."

"Nah, I'd rather not." Karen, who was a timid rider since her bad riding accident last year, was comfortable riding her lazy Morgan mare but hesitant to try new things such as driving. Heather didn't want to force Karen, so she decided to go by herself. Heading into the tack room to grab the tiny harness, Heather set to work getting the little horse ready. Once the harness was properly adjusted, Rerun was led outside to be hitched to the cart.

As she was attaching the leather parts to the buggy, Heather noticed Rerun was unusually restless. "Take it easy, girl. It'll only take me a minute."

But Rerun wanted to go. She pulled at the bit and pawed at the wet ground. Feeling a need to rush, Heather finished hooking the harness to the cart and hopped aboard. She guided Rerun to the road and headed down towards the dirt section, the same area where she and Nicholas had been practicing the road trot the day before.

Rerun certainly wanted to get going. Usually it took a few minutes for the horse to wake up, but today she wanted to trot. "Not yet, Rerun. You need to warm up first. Slow down," commanded Heather as she pulled on the reins harder than she liked. Rerun threw her head up and fought the pressure. "What's wrong, Rerun?" asked Heather, trying to figure out why the horse was being so bad.

Deciding the mare must have more built-up energy than usual, perhaps from being confined to her stall, Heather finally stopped worrying. Slowly, the mare settled down and began to walk.

When they reached the unpaved section of road, Heather gave Rerun the cue to trot. The mare readily broke into a fast trot, much like the record-breaking road trot that made the judge take notice last year when Chauncy drove her at a show. Passing many of the full-sized horses, Rerun easily won that class. Unlike her show ring performance however, where the horse's head-set was absolutely perfect, her ears pricked forward in happy obedience, and her speed controlled by Chauncy's experienced hands, this drive was not a pretty picture. Rerun's head moved all over the place, up, down, and off to the side as she tried to evade the bit. Her ears slanted backwards to show her irritability, and her speed was uncontrolled—fast, faster, and fastest.

Mud splattered up onto Rerun's white belly. A few icy patches hidden under the mud caused her little legs to slip. The somewhat inexperienced driver tried to convince the horse to use caution, but Rerun didn't care. She simply wanted to go fast.

It didn't take long before Rerun, out of shape from a winter of easy living, began to pant. But still she didn't want to stop. Pulling harder on the reins, Heather struggled to get the mare to stop. "Come on, Rerun. You've got to take it easy. I know you want to run, but you're going to get sick if you go so fast. Whoa, girl, whoa."

Rerun fought to keep going but her driver persisted and was finally able to get the mare to walk. As they moved along at a comfortable speed, Heather noticed steam rising from the mare's sides. Realizing the mare had broken a sweat and that her extra thick winter coat was wet, Heather decided it was time to head home. It would take a long time to cool the horse out, and she wanted to rub the mare down with a towel to help dry her out.

Heather kept Rerun walking down the road until she could find a spot wide enough to allow for a turn. She needed to find a large, open area to make it easy on the horse to reverse directions while pulling a cart. A few minutes later she located a place on the side of the road where people often parked their cars so they could enjoy the view of meandering fields. Heather guided Rerun to the outcropping created by the cars and began to turn the mare. Rerun immediately realized they were turning and heading home, and she picked up a trot without being told. Heather once again pulled on the reins but the mare ignored her.

Turning sharply, Rerun started to charge toward home. But then, halfway through the turn, the mare erupted in violent bucking. Heather screamed in terror. The frightened girl didn't have time to think, only react.

Rerun reared straight up, her head flying into the air. She went so high that Heather thought the horse was going to flip over and land on her. But then the mare went down. Without stopping, the angry horse lowered her head to the ground as she flung her back feet up. Coming within inches of the metal footrest, Rerun's hooves continued up toward Heather's face. The horrified girl instinctively ducked as she thought she was about to get kicked. Next the mare reared up again, as high as her small stature would allow, almost losing her balance as she threw her front legs out. Pounding back to the ground, her back feet kicked out at Heather, but this time they made contact with the cart. This terrified both girl and horse and resulted in more bucking. Rerun tried to charge ahead, full-speed, while still bucking.

Heather didn't know what to do. "Whoa, Rerun, whoa!" she screamed as she dug her feet into the footrest for added strength and pulled back on the reins as hard as she could. "Please! Stop!"

Rerun rose into the air again, her mouth wide open as she fought the bit. She tried to buck and run at the same time, but with the reins pulled back tightly, her head was held close to her chest. Unable to swing her head out and up, she couldn't get enough momentum to rear, so instead she bounced, fought, and ran. "Stop!" pleaded Heather as she continued to pull. Raising her body up slightly in the cart, she leaned back while she braced herself with her legs straining against the footrest. This allowed her to pull even harder on the reins, which finally forced Rerun to stop.

Without hesitating, Heather jumped out of the cart and ran to Rerun's head. She didn't know what to make of Rerun's odd behavior. Immediately she saw that the horse was shaking. "Rerun?" she asked, uncertain of what was going on. She stroked the mare's neck while Rerun looked around as if searching for something that had frightened her. That was when Heather realized that she too was trembling. "What was that all about?"

Rerun shook her head and pushed against Heather's body, asking to run back home. "I don't get it," the girl told herself. "You acted like you got stung by a bee or something, but it's too early in the year for bees. What's bothering you?"

Heather stood next to the Miniature Horse and stroked her neck and back. She was trying to calm the mare down, but really, she was trying to calm herself down too. Patting the horse definitely helped Heather feel better.

"Whoa, Rerun, whoa!"

Running her hand along Rerun's back, she suddenly felt a strange bump. It was on the mare's left side, slightly off from the center of her spine. It was the size of a person's fist but with all of the horse's winter fuzz, it was hard to notice. "What's this?" asked Heather. The frightened girl took her gloves off and felt carefully around the bump, looking for the spot where it began and ended. Then, gently feeling the center, she watched Rerun's reaction as she slowly applied a little pressure. Rerun's ears went back as she flinched and kicked out with a hind foot. "That hurts you, doesn't it?"

Trying to figure out if the bump was the cause of Rerun's dangerous behavior, Heather cautiously took the reins and walked around to the back of the buggy. Clucking to the horse, the girl walked behind the buggy, not daring to enter and sit down. Rerun was agitated but she didn't buck. "I wonder if . . ." her voice trailed off. Asking the mare to reverse directions, the horse obeyed until, once again, she was about halfway through the turn. At this point, Heather noticed the harness strap that ran down the center of Rerun's back to the tailpiece move slightly. The movement was just enough to place the leather strap directly over the bump.

Rerun erupted into another violent bucking episode. She reared up, tossed her head, and tried to run away, but Heather was ready this time with her feet firmly planted in the muddy road. With a little effort, she was able to stop the horse.

Once the mare was standing still, Heather ran to the horse's head to soothe the frightened animal. "Easy, girl. Easy. We'll get this figured out."

Heather slipped the reins through the harness loops and folded the long leather reins in her hands. She removed the cart from the harness and took the many leather pieces off the horse. Placing the harness on the footrest, Heather left the cart behind as she and the frightened horse began the long walk home.

"Oh, Heather, there you are!" exclaimed Chauncy as he emerged from his house. "I finally got a letter from Mrs. Collins. We have another lead on Annie's mysterious past . . ." Chauncy's voice trailed off. He knew something was wrong instantly.

Heather was leading Rerun towards the barn. The Miniature Horse had her harness bridle on, but not the harness. "Where's the cart?" asked Chauncy, noticing the missing buggy.

Heather looked at her mentor but didn't say anything for a moment. Then she began, "We had a little, um, accident that—"

"What happened?" interrupted Chauncy as he dashed to his friend's side. He could tell Heather was upset. "Are you hurt? Did Rerun bolt?"

"No, I'm fine, really. Rerun was acting really weird today; she was frisky, but also really, really angry. She wouldn't listen to me and wanted to run. I had to pull hard to keep her under control. When it was time to return, she freaked out and started bucking. I was able to stop her and jumped out of the cart. But when I was trying to calm her down, I noticed a bump on her back. Look." Heather showed Chauncy the strange growth on Rerun's back.

"That's bizarre," he concluded after examining it. "I've never seen anything like it."

"If you push on it, it hurts," explained Heather as she gently applied pressure to the area. "See?"

Rerun lowered her back, trying to get away from the pain. Stomping a front foot and swishing her tail, Rerun tried to push past Chauncy and Heather.

"What's wrong?" asked Karen. She had been riding Robin in the ring but dismounted and came into the yard when she saw Heather and Rerun approach.

Not wanting to upset her friend, Heather brushed off her own frightening experience. "Oh, nothing. Rerun has some sort of bump on her back, and I was showing it to Chauncy."

"Where?"

"Right here. See?" asked Heather as she ran her hand over Rerun's back.

"I don't see anything," said Karen, who was holding Robin and couldn't get very close.

"I'll watch Robin so you can look," offered Heather. Grabbing the Morgan's reins, she continued, "Run your hand gently over Rerun's back. Right there."

"I still don't feel it," said a frustrated Karen.

"Take your gloves off," suggested Heather. "There's so much winter hair in the way it's hard to find."

Doing as she was told, Karen felt the bump for the first time. "Chauncy? What is it?"

"I don't know, Karen. But I think it's time to call the vet."

The following day was extremely cold and windy, not a good day for riding. Karen arrived at the barn with her dad a few minutes after school ended. She normally took the bus, but with the vet coming, she wanted to be there early. Mr. Greene was happy to drive his daughter to Chauncy's house. He hadn't seen his old friend for several weeks and wanted to catch up on what was new with the horseman. Of course, he was also very concerned about Rerun and wanted her to receive the best care possible.

By the time Heather's bus dropped her off, Karen, her father, and Chauncy had already been to the barn, visited with all the horses, and gone to the house to wait for Dr. Reilly, the veterinarian. Heather also went to the barn first where she greeted each horse, gave them all carrots, and then headed to the house. As she was about to walk up the steps to the front door, Dr. Reilly pulled into the driveway in his red pickup truck.

"He's here," loudly announced Heather as she popped into the house. Dashing back out, she headed to the vet's truck. "Hi, Dr. Reilly."

"Heather! How are you?"

"Pretty good, I guess. I had a pretty scary driving incident yesterday."

"Chauncy told me all about it."

"Hi, Dr. Reilly," greeted Karen as she, her father, and Chauncy approached.

"Hey, Karen. Good to see you again. I hear you've got a problem with Rerun."

"Yeah, I think she hurt herself."

"Well, why don't you bring her into the barn aisle and I'll take a look."

Karen led the way into the barn with everyone else silently following her. Haltering her little friend and leading her out of the stall, Karen spoke softly to Rerun. Dr. Reilly bent over the tiny horse and studied her back. "Right there," said Karen, pointing to the troubling spot.

"I see it," said Dr. Reilly. Slowly running his hands over the area on the back, he mumbled, "Hmm . . . that's strange." Watching the mare's reaction, he noted, "It doesn't seem to be bothering her." But when he applied a bit of pressure, Rerun flinched and stomped her left front foot.

"See?" asked Heather. "It does hurt her. And when I was driving her, she was okay until I asked her to turn and the harness strap went right over that spot."

"Well," guessed Dr. Reilly as he stood up, "the pain may have been caused by the strap or by the motion of her turning. It could be some sort of soft tissue lesion that is pressing against her spine."

"Will it get worse?" asked Heather.

"I don't know," answered Dr. Reilly. "First we have to figure out what it is."

"What's a soft tissue lesion?" asked a very concerned Karen.

"It could be a cyst, which is a pocket filled with fluid or it could be a soft tissue swelling due to trauma, a tumor, or a possible infection."

"A pocket filled with fluid? Ew, gross," replied Karen. "Can you pop it and get the gunk out?"

"It all depends on what this is and what's inside," answered Dr. Reilly. "Where are your clippers?" he asked Chauncy.

"I'll get them," replied Heather as she darted off to the tack room. Returning a moment later, she plugged the clippers into a wall socket and handed them to the doctor. He carefully trimmed the hair from the area surrounding the raised bump on Rerun's back and gave the clippers back to Heather.

"That looks better," noted Dr. Reilly. "I could never see anything with all that hair in the way."

Feeling the site again, he continued, "Hold on a minute," and headed back to his truck. A minute later the veterinarian returned, took off his winter hat and slipped on a pair of odd looking glasses. The sides of the glasses were dark blue, and there was a strap that held them in place on the doctor's head. Attached to the glasses was a long, black wire that ran down to a box-like contraption wrapped around Dr. Reilly's waist. Another black wire went from the box to a wand-like handle. Holding the handle with one hand, Dr. Reilly used the other hand to apply a clear, goopy substance to Rerun's back.

"What's that?" asked Karen, looking at the wand.

"This strange looking device is a portable ultrasound. It will allow me to see below Rerun's skin so we can hopefully figure out what is going on."

Dr. Reilly touched the wand to Rerun's back. The cute little mare didn't seem to feel anything, as she was busy chomping on a clump of hay Heather had given her. The vet moved the wand back and forth through the clear goop he had applied to the area. "There is definitely something under the skin, although I'm not sure what it is. Do you want to see it?" he asked Karen as he removed the glasses from his head.

"Sure, I guess so," replied the girl, uncertain of what she was doing.

"Here, put these glasses on," instructed Dr. Reilly as he helped place the funny looking glasses on

Karen. Placing the wand on Rerun's back, he said, "Can you see it now?"

"I don't see anything. Oh, wait, there's um, a blob?"

Dr. Reilly smiled and moved the wand a bit. "How about now?"

"It looks kinda like a bubble."

"That's it."

"Can I see?" asked Heather.

"Here," said Karen as she handed the glasses to Heather.

"It doesn't look like much," decided Heather as she concentrated on the gray mass in front of her eyes. "How can you tell what it is?"

"My guess is that it is a cyst of some sort," concluded Dr. Reilly.

"What do we do now?" asked Mr. Greene who had been silently watching the examination.

"I don't have the expertise or facilities to work on something like this," admitted Dr. Reilly. "I think the next step is to make an appointment with the University Clinic in Westfield. They're set up to handle situations like this."

"They're the ones who operated on Shadow when her legs got crooked," noted Heather. "Don't worry Karen, they were really good with Shadow when she had to have an operation," said Heather, trying her best to ease Karen's worry. But all the young girl heard was the word 'operation.'

"An operation?" she asked, fixed on that frightening word.

"Rerun's problem isn't that serious, is it Dr. Reilly? She won't need any surgery," encouraged Heather.

"I don't think so Heather, but the clinic will have to tell you that, not me. If you'd like, Mr. Greene, I can call them when I return to my office later this afternoon and make an appointment."

"I think that's a good idea," said Mr. Greene. Pulling out his wallet, Karen's father handed the vet a business card and continued, "Call me at this number as soon as you hear back from the clinic. We want to do whatever we can to help Rerun."

Heather, who was standing next to Karen, wrapped her arm around the girl and whispered, "Rerun will be fine, I promise." But still, all Karen heard was 'operation.' As Karen's heart sank, Rerun pushed her fuzzy head against the girl's jacket, looking for a treat. "I'm sorry, girl," responded Karen. "I'll get you a peppermint." But instead she bent down and hugged her tiny friend as a tear ran down her cheek.

THE MYSTERY DEEPENS

"Oh, there you are," said Chauncy as he strolled into the barn early Saturday morning.

"Hi Chauncy," replied Heather. She was busy grooming Shadow who was dancing around in place on the cross ties. The young filly was also trying to grab the cotton ties with her lips, unable to keep still. "What's up?"

"I started to tell you the other day," he began, referring to the day Heather returned to the barn leading a frightened Rerun, "that I finally heard from Mrs. Collins."

"Mrs. Who?"

"Mrs. Collins, the woman who sold Annie to Mrs. Patrick."

"Oh, yeah. I guess it's getting kind of confusing."

Chauncy smiled. "Anyway, it took two letters, but I finally heard back."

"Please tell me her name isn't Cookie."

Chauncy rolled his eyes.

"Oh, no!" exclaimed Heather. "Her name is Cookie! Ugh!"

"Well," chuckled Chauncy, "as far as I'm concerned, her name is now Annie."

"Annie? Really, Chauncy? Are you sure?" asked Heather.

"Yes," replied Chauncy. "Annie is a much better name. Anyway," he continued, "Mrs. Collins bought the mare from a horse trader up in Maine. I've tracked that person down and he told me that he bought Annie at a local auction."

"An auction? In Maine?" asked Heather. She didn't like the sound of that.

"Yup, afraid so," confirmed Chauncy.

"Did you call the auction house?"

"Yes," continued Chauncy. "I talked to one of the owners, but without a date of sale, registered name of the horse, or the name of the person who sold the horse, they couldn't help me. I gave them the name Cookie but that didn't help. I'm guessing the name was given to the mare by Mrs. Collins. Without any idea of when the mare went through the auction, they couldn't help."

"What about the horse trader?" asked Heather. "Doesn't he know when he bought the mare from the auction? He should be able to track down the sale date, especially since we know it's the mare he sold to Mrs. Collins."

"I tried," admitted Chauncy. "But the guy wasn't very helpful. It sounded like his paperwork wasn't very good, maybe even nonexistent. And he was just plain grumpy."

"What now?"

"Well, I think I'll be taking a ride up to Maine. The man I spoke to at the auction said I was welcome to come up and go through their sales receipts. I might be able to find a receipt for a horse that fits Annie's description. But they're not willing to take the time to do it, so I've got to do it myself."

"Can I come?" impatiently asked Heather.

"I don't think so."

"But I don't mind the long car ride up to Maine," pleaded Heather.

"Oh, I know that, Heather. You've always been a great travel companion. But the gentleman at the auction house told me if I wanted to look through all their receipts, I'd have to come during the week when there's not much going on."

"They don't have an auction every weekend, do they?"

"I think they have one every few weeks. They also apparently have a lesson program and a couple of trainers working out of the same barn, so it gets very busy on the weekends. I'll be heading up either on Monday or Tuesday, and you'll be in school."

"Oh," mumbled a disappointed Heather. "But I don't mind missing a day of school."

"I know you don't," smiled Chauncy, "but I bet your parents wouldn't be too happy."

"Bummer." Heather knew Chauncy was right, but she still would have loved to help find clues to Annie's past.

"Why don't you show me how Annie is going under saddle?" suggested Chauncy. He knew Heather was getting attached to the cute chestnut mare and was pleased with the progress they had been making. Just as she had done with both Frosty and Blackjack, Heather was turning a nervous, frightened horse into a trusted friend. He only hoped he could get to the bottom of Annie's hidden past.

Rerun's appointment at the University Clinic in Westfield was on Saturday morning. At 8 a.m. sharp, Karen, Heather, and Nicholas, having loaded Rerun into the trailer moments before, piled into the back seat of Chauncy's pickup truck. Mr. Greene and Chauncy then got into the front, and the whole crew set off for Westfield.

The backseat was cramped, so the kids' legs were scrunched up towards their chests, but they didn't mind; they were too busy talking. Heather had told Karen several times about how wonderful the clinic was, what a great job they had done correcting Shadow's crooked legs, and how nice everybody who worked there had been to her. She also tried to cheer Karen up by telling her Shadow's reason for visiting the clinic was far more serious than Rerun's, that the young foal had actually needed surgery. Rerun, she figured, would only need some medicine. Whether or not Karen believed her, Heather didn't know, but both she and Nicholas encouraged Karen not to worry; everything would be fine. After a few minutes of clinic talk, they chatted up a storm about horse shows, doing their best to keep Karen's mind off Rerun's problem.

Arriving at the clinic an hour later, Chauncy instructed the three friends to wait while he and Mr. Greene went inside and got instructions on where to go. Heather and Nicholas continued talking about the time Heather showed Rusty up in Maine in a huge jumping class. "The one with the fake moose, remember?" asked Heather.

"Oh, yeah! How could I forget?" giggled Nicholas, remembering the funny moose who frightened many horses on the course. "Karen, you should have seen it!" exclaimed Nicholas. But Karen was staring out the window, watching her dad walk away.

Seeing her friend's anxiety, Heather suggested, "Let's check on Rerun."

"But Chauncy said to stay in the truck," protested Karen.

"It's okay," explained Heather. "As long as we don't stray away from the truck, Chauncy won't mind."

"Heather is right," added Nicholas. "Chauncy said to wait here, and we're waiting here. We're just going to the back of the truck. And besides, it's a good thing to check on Rerun."

Heather, Nicholas, and Karen unlocked their seatbelts, exited the truck, and walked to the side of the trailer. Peering through the small window, Heather saw Rerun munching happily on her hay. "She's fine," whispered Heather.

"What are you kids doing outside the truck?" asked Mr. Greene as he approached.

"We wanted to see if Rerun was okay."

"Chauncy asked you to stay in the truck," scolded Mr. Greene.

"Sorry, Dad," replied Karen.

Heather felt guilty for suggesting they check on Rerun. "It's my fault," she admitted. "I thought it would keep Karen's mind off stuff."

Chauncy understood, but still, they were in a strange place and he didn't want anybody wandering around. "Okay, Heather, thanks for acknowledging that it was your idea. Let's not do it again, all right?"

"Yes, Chauncy. Sorry."

"We're supposed to go to Area 3, Prep stall 8," said Chauncy, changing the subject. "It's around the side of the building, so hop back into the truck."

As they drove around to the side, Heather saw a section marked Area 2. "That's where Shadow had to go!" she told everybody. "I wonder why we're going to a different section?"

"I think because Area 2 is for surgery patients. Area 3 is probably for simpler cases," guessed Chauncy.

"Oh," replied Heather. "See, Karen? We're going to the place for easy cases. Just some medicine and we'll be out of here," encouraged Heather.

Arriving at the designated spot, Chauncy parked the truck and everybody hopped out. "Karen, why don't you go in the trailer and untie Rerun?"

"Okay, Chauncy," said Karen as she silently walked up to the trailer door and opened it.

"All set?" asked Chauncy after a few moments.

"Yup, she's untied."

Chauncy lowered the trailer ramp and stepped aside. There was no butt strap to undo this time, as the little horse was too small to be stopped by a metal bar that ran at the height of a typical horse's rump. Instead, Chauncy had placed several bales of hay around Rerun to protect her. The Miniature Horse followed her owner out of the trailer and immediately spotted a small clump of grass growing between cracks in the cement driveway. She pulled at her lead rope but Karen pulled right back. "No Rerun, this way!" she demanded.

"You must be Karen and this must be Rerun," said a husky young man in a white lab coat. "My name is Jake Lambert and I'll be assisting Dr. Kent today." Looking at Nicholas, he guessed, "You're Karen's brother?"

"No, just a friend. My name's Nicholas."

"Pleased to meet you, Nicholas." Turning to face Heather and Chauncy, Jake smiled and continued, "Hannah?"

"No, it's Heather."

"Of course," cheerily replied Jake. "And Chauncy, right? Let's see . . . you brought in a weanling with crooked legs."

"Yes! That's Shadow, one of my horses. You remember her?"

"Of course I do," replied Jake. "I remember almost all our cases. So, how is Shadow doing?"

"Great!" answered Heather. "She's a yearling now and you can't tell there was ever anything wrong with her."

"That's fantastic! We've had really good results with surgeries like hers. I'm glad Shadow did so well, too." Turning his attention back to Karen, Jake continued, "You can lead Rerun in through that door."

Karen saw a huge door, much like a common garage door, wide open. Underneath it stood two women, each about twenty years old and also dressed in white lab coats. Jake led the way with

Karen following closely behind, leading her tiny horse into the building.

"Hello, Karen," said one of the women. "My name is Tina and my friend is Joan. We're Dr. Kent's assistants and we'll be with Rerun all day."

"Hi," was all Karen could muster.

"This must be our patient," came a new voice. Everybody turned to see yet another woman in a white lab coat. She was in her early thirties, with black hair and pretty silver earrings. Heather recognized her instantly; it was Dr. Kent, the veterinarian who had operated on Shadow. "I'm Dr. Kent and you must be Karen," she said, holding out her hand.

Karen shook the doctor's hand and meekly replied, "Yes, that's me."

"And I'm her dad, Bob Greene," added her father as he held out one hand to shake the doctor's hand and rested his other around his daughter's shoulder.

"Yes, of course. It's a pleasure to meet you both. And you're Karen's brother?" asked the doctor, looking at Nicholas.

Heather giggled. Poor Nicholas, everybody thought he was Karen's brother. "No, I'm just a friend."

"Well, she's lucky to have such a good friend." Looking at Chauncy, she continued, "Mr. Campbell, it's a pleasure to see you again; and Heather too. Well, I guess we've got the whole group from Gallant Morgans here. By the way, how is Shadow? I talked to Dr. Reilly several months ago and heard she was doing fine."

"She's made a full recovery," confirmed Chauncy.

"I'm so glad to hear that. Now, I hear we've got something a little different today," said Dr. Kent as she turned her attention to Rerun. "Dr. Reilly faxed me a copy of his report. We have a lump of some sort on her back?"

"Right here," said Karen as she placed her hand on Rerun's back.

Dr. Kent bent down and ran her hands along Rerun's spine. Rerun turned her head to see what was going on. Noticing the Miniature's curiosity, Dr. Kent slipped one hand into her coat pocket and pulled out a baby carrot. She offered it to Rerun, who instantly made the carrot disappear. Immediately, Rerun nudged the doctor, asking for more. Everybody smiled. "You sure know how to gain a fat little pony's trust," laughed Nicholas.

Dr. Kent returned her hands to Rerun's back. "There's definitely an edematous swelling at the left dorsal lumbar area."

"Huh?" asked Karen.

"I'm sorry. A lump on her back. Karen?" asked the doctor as she straightened up.

"Yes?"

"I'd like to do a lameness test first. Can you lead Rerun outside for me?"

"Okay." Karen led Rerun back through the big door into the morning sun with everybody else following closely behind.

"Walk her down the driveway a bit," instructed Dr. Kent. Karen did as told, with Rerun obediently walking beside her. "Okay, that's far enough. Now turn slowly and walk back toward me. Good. Now do it again, but this time at a trot." Karen started running, forcing Rerun into a trot. The little horse trotted down the road, then back to the building. "Good, very good, Karen. She needs to stand still for a minute now, while I hold her leg up." Dr. Kent gently took Rerun's left hind leg and held it up in the air, while keeping an eye on her watch. "As soon as I let go of her leg, you need to make her trot. Can you do that, Karen? Immediately, okay?"

"Yes."

"As soon as I tell you . . . now, Karen, trot her!"

Karen clucked to Rerun and pulled on the lead rope. Rerun didn't want to trot and resisted. After one stride, however, she broke into a trot. Dr. Kent watched carefully as the mare moved down the road. "Bring her back." When Karen returned, Dr. Kent instructed, "We're going to do the exact same thing, but this time with the right hind leg." She took the other back leg and held it up, once again watching the time. "Same thing, now, Karen. You need to trot her off quickly."

"Okay."

"Now!" ordered Dr. Kent as she let go of the leg. Rerun, having figured out that she was expected to run, willingly broke into a trot, tossing her head in excitement. "That's far enough. You can come back now." In a few moments, Karen and Rerun were standing next to Dr. Kent. "That was very good," reassured Dr. Kent.

"Is she okay? Is she lame?" asked Karen, anxious for an answer.

"No, she's not lame," replied the doctor. "Nothing wrong with her legs, so we can rule that out as the root of the problem. Let's head inside for the rest of the exam."

Once inside, Tina gently took the lead rope from Karen and led the Miniature Horse down a hallway, past several stalls, and into a darkened room. Jake flipped a switch and the room was instantly flooded in light. The other assistant, Joan, grabbed a pair of clippers and began to trim the same area Dr. Reilly had clipped not long before. She cut a perfect rectangle, and the hair was so short that the bump was now easy to see. Next, she created an identically shaped box on the other side of Rerun's spine. "But there's nothing wrong on that side," complained Karen.

"We know," said Joan. "But it helps the doctor to compare the damaged area to a similar area that hasn't been affected."

"Oh."

"We're going to take some x-rays now," explained Tina. "You'll have to leave the room. Don't worry; it won't hurt her a bit and will only take a few minutes."

The group from Gallant Morgans left the room and wandered over to a small reception area. Heather and Nicholas strolled over to one of the walls covered with pictures of recent patients. Many of the photos showed horses as they came into the clinic, injured, skinny, or with head hanging in obvious pain. All of the after pictures showed frisky horses with sleek coats and happy owners.

"You can come back now," said Tina as she popped her head into the waiting room. "We're all set."

The Greenes and their friends followed the assistant back to the prep room where Rerun was chomping on another carrot. Karen gave her horse a big hug in an effort to calm the mare but Rerun didn't need any reassuring; she was perfectly happy, and in fact, seemed to be enjoying all the attention. "Karen, would you come into my office, please?" asked Dr. Kent as she entered the room.

The group followed the doctor down a hallway and into a small room, cluttered with a large desk and a lot of paper. In the middle of the desk was a computer with an unusual picture on the screen. "What's that?" asked Karen. Heather and Nicholas peered over their friend's shoulder.

"That's one of Rerun's x-rays," said Dr. Kent, who was now sitting at her desk.

Karen couldn't figure out what she was seeing. The top third of the screen was black, while the lower section was off-white with strange lines and shades of gray throughout. "Right there? Is that her lump?" asked Karen, pointing to a blob of gray shapes.

"No, that's her intestines. This here," corrected Dr. Kent, picking up a pen and pointing to a spot on the screen.

Karen looked above the intestines. "Are those pointy things her backbone?"

"Yes, that's it."

"Oh! I see it!" exclaimed Heather from behind Karen. "Look Karen, there."

But Karen still didn't see it. "I can't tell the difference."

"It's okay, Karen. Sometimes these things can be pretty hard to see. The good news is that it doesn't look like there is anything interfering with Rerun's spine. No tumor or fractures." Looking straight at Karen, Dr. Kent repeated, "That's very good news, Karen. The next step is to do an ultrasound, so let's head back to Rerun."

"But Dr. Reilly already did one," protested Karen.

"I know," answered the doctor. "But our equipment is more sensitive and may pick up something that Dr. Reilly's portable ultrasound missed."

Everybody stepped aside so the doctor could lead the way. They returned to Rerun who was enjoying a scratch from Jake. Dr. Kent sat down on a chair with wheels, while Joan rolled a small table over to Rerun's side. "Many horses have to have a mild sedative for this step because we need them to be perfectly still," explained Dr. Kent. "But I don't think that will be a problem with Rerun. We'll keep feeding her carrots."

The table held a machine that looked a lot like a computer. Karen guessed it must be the ultrasound. Dr. Kent wheeled her chair over to the table, turned the contraption on, then picked up what looked like a tube of toothpaste and squeezed some of its clear contents onto Rerun's back. "This gel helps us get a better view. What we'll see on the screen is not a picture of Rerun's insides like we saw with the x-rays, but rather an image created by sound waves. An ultrasound works by bouncing sound off different objects, of different densities. Hopefully, it will give us a little insight into Rerun's lump."

Joan dimmed the lights in the room and the doctor got to work. She picked up a wand, much like the one Dr. Reilly had used with his portable ultrasound, and ran it along the shaved section of Rerun's back. She checked both sides of the horse's back, the one with the bump and the unaffected side. Finally, she quietly noted, perhaps more to herself than to the group watching, "There is definitely an enlarged and edematous swelling of the dorsal spinal ligament." Then it was silent again while the doctor viewed more samples from the ultrasound. Meanwhile, Rerun stood perfectly still, only moving her head and lips looking for carrots. Every few minutes, Joan or Tina fed the horse a treat to keep the mare from getting upset and moving around. Finally, Dr. Kent pulled herself away from the ultrasound table and looked up at Mr. Greene and his daughter. "I'd say we're looking at a chronic desmitis of the dorsal spinal ligament; in layman's terms, a chronic inflammation. There is fluid build-up in the area and if you press it," Dr. Kent placed her thumb on the spot and pressed hard while Rerun shifted her weight and stomped her back foot, "it changes. See how the swelling appears to have gone down?" she asked as she removed her thumb.

Karen was amazed to see the bump get smaller. "Is that all we have to do to get rid of it?"

"No, unfortunately not. All I'm actually doing is moving the fluid around. It's not going away. In a few moments the fluid will return to the same spot and the bump will appear to grow back to its previous size."

"So what caused it and how do we get rid of it?" asked Chauncy, hoping for a cure.

"I can't say what caused it. It could have been from a kick, a fall, perhaps Rerun was bucking and twisted her back and pulled a muscle. Whatever it was, it caused an inflammation that never cleared up. It's now become a chronic, or persistent, inflammation that continually feeds upon itself; it won't go away on its own."

"Is she in pain?" asked Karen.

"No, I don't believe so."

"Then why did she freak out when I was driving her?" asked Heather.

"I'm not sure," admitted Dr. Kent. "It might have been from the harness strap rubbing against the bump, or perhaps the act of turning pushed the fluid against her spine."

"Will we ever be able to drive her again?" questioned Chauncy.

"I think so. You can drive her without the breeching strap, right?"

"Show harnesses don't use breeching, so I suppose we could do the same."

"I'd try that and keep things easy. Just walking at first; see how she reacts," suggested Dr. Kent.

"Will the bump go away?" This time it was Mr. Greene's turn to ask a question.

"There's no way to know. I'm going to give you some ointment that you'll need to rub into Rerun's skin twice a day, as well as Bute, which is a powder you'll add to her grain. Both of these medications are anti-inflammatories. Hopefully, the combination will lessen the amount of fluid."

"Can't you just give her some pills that will make the bump go away?" asked Karen.

"I'm afraid there's no magic pill for this, Karen."

Karen's heart sank. She thought the doctor, with all the fancy equipment and medicine at her disposal, would be able to cure Rerun. Instead, all she was given was some medicine that might make Rerun better, or might not. What would she do if Rerun's bump never went away?

FINDING CLUES

Every morning after feeding, Chauncy applied a small amount of the ointment Dr. Kent had prescribed to Rerun's back. In the evenings, Karen repeated the procedure and also gave her Miniature Horse a measured scoop of Bute. Fortunately, unlike Rusty who absolutely hated anything added to his grain, Rerun licked her bucket clean at every feeding. The medicine was easy to get into Rerun, but after three weeks, Karen hadn't seen any improvement. "I don't think it's working," she told Chauncy one afternoon.

"Hmm . . ." mumbled Chauncy as he wandered over to Rerun on the cross ties. "You may be right. There doesn't seem to be any change."

"What's up?" asked Heather, walking into the barn with Blackjack.

"I don't think Rerun is getting better."

Blackjack grunted a greeting to Rerun. Holding the stallion's head away from the Miniature Horse, Heather bent over and looked at the gray and white mare. "You're right. The bump hasn't gotten any smaller."

"Dr. Kent did say the medicine might not work," said Chauncy. Seeing Karen's disappointment, he continued, "But that doesn't mean you can't still have fun with Rerun."

"What will I do with her if we can't drive her? She'll be miserable."

"That's not true, Karen," disagreed Chauncy. "The doctor said the fluid wasn't hurting her; that Rerun isn't in pain. You can still lunge her, you can take her out on trail rides by riding Robin and leading her, and you can turn her out in the pasture with Robin. She is Robin's best friend and that makes her special."

"You're right, Chauncy. I know I shouldn't be so disappointed. It's just that I want her to be normal."

"But this may be normal for Rerun now. Your job is to love her, give her lots of treats, see that she's taken care of, and keep her stall clean!"

The comment about keeping Rerun's stall clean made Karen giggle. She was always groaning about how such a tiny horse could make such a big mess. "Okay, Chauncy, I promise to love Rerun forever."

Saturday morning Heather was in the barn tacking Blackjack up for his training session. Frosty had already been brushed and had her saddle on waiting for Nicholas to arrive. She was in her stall, munching hay, with the girth loosely hooked around her belly. "What took you so long?" asked Heather when Nicholas finally arrived.

Jumping off Spot, he replied, "Spot was being a pain this morning and wouldn't let me catch him."

"Well, Frosty is all set. She just needs her bridle."

"Great, I'll be right back." Nicholas led Spot out to the ring where he slipped the brightly colored gelding's tack off and let the horse loose. Locking the gate, he returned to the barn and finished getting Frosty ready.

As the two friends were mounting their horses, Laura, Chauncy's daughter, appeared from the house.

"Laura! I didn't know you were home this weekend!" exclaimed Heather.

"Didn't Dad tell you? The weather was supposed to be so nice that I had to come home and ride. I haven't seen the horses in a while, and I wanted to check out Dad's new mare too."

"Isn't she cute?"

"Yeah, she's really nice. I hope Dad can get her papers."

"Are you going to ride Rusty today?"

"I was thinking of trying Annie," answered Laura.

"She's pretty easy to ride, but she tends to jig a lot in the ring."

"Where are you guys going?"

"Down the road. I need to practice Blackjack's road trot for the Justin Morgan class."

"Oh! Can I come?" exclaimed Laura. "I love trotting races!"

"Sure! We'll take it easy so you can get used to Annie."

It didn't take long for Laura to get Annie brushed and saddled. Then the friends were off, headed down Mill Creek Road.

The March mud had dried up and green grass was starting to pop up along the roadside. Laura told Nicholas and Heather all about the courses she was taking at college, the part-time job she had, and about the college riding team she had joined. Annie behaved wonderfully, easily adjusting to her new rider. She seemed happy, with ears forward and a quick snap to her walk. "Are you ready to try trotting?" asked Heather once the horses were warmed up.

"Sure, Annie seems fine," replied Laura. As an experienced rider who had won many trophies with lots of horses, Laura was an excellent judge of equines. If she was comfortable riding Annie, Heather wasn't worried.

Laura and Nicholas clucked to their horses at the same time. Frosty instantly broke into a trot while Annie hesitated, but only for a moment. As soon as she saw the gray mare speed up, she was eager to follow. Blackjack, too, wanted to go but he obediently waited for the cue from his owner. Heather wanted to give the others a head start so Blackjack would have more of a challenge. He was fast and needed to race horses who would push him; make him work hard. If Heather didn't give the others an advantage, there would probably be no real race.

Blackjack continued to walk but not happily. He tossed his head and started to jig. His step got snappy, something he did when he wanted to run. "Okay, Blackjack, you can go now." Heather loosened the reins a tiny bit and her horse was off.

Instead of lowering his head as he dashed along, Blackjack kept it raised, ears forward, and nose only slightly out. But as he closed in on his rivals, his ears tilted back. The joy of competition was in Blackjack's blood, and he loved pursuing and over-taking other horses. Heather too, absolutely loved racing her stallion. She felt like she was flying, her hair blowing back underneath her helmet and her eyes tearing from the wind blowing past them.

Heather was surprised to see Annie keeping up with Frosty. She had never tried trotting the chest-nut mare at speed and didn't know how fast she could go. Frosty, she knew, loved to trot fast out on the trails and could zoom through the woods, dodg-ing branches and tree roots as though they didn't exist.

Twice Annie broke into a canter and Laura was forced to pull back on the reins to slow her down to a trot. Annie didn't want to stop cantering and fought her rider, but Laura knew how to control an overly anxious horse. Instead of snapping at Annie, Laura talked to her in a soothing voice and gently pulled at the reins. "She's pretty good," she told Heather as the black stallion caught up.

"But you'll never catch us!" dared Nicholas, who was a few strides ahead of the others.

Blackjack did catch up to Frosty, but amazingly, so too did Annie. "Look at her go!" gleefully hollered Heather, astonished at Annie's speed. "Yee-ha!"

Heather and her horse inched forward and did manage to get the lead, but it wasn't easy. Frosty was fast and it appeared Annie was too.

It was an amazing feeling as the horses pushed forward, trying to get in front of their barnmates. All three riders intently concentrated on their horses, using their legs to encourage speed while guiding their animals' direction with their hands. Keeping the horses from breaking into a canter was also done with their hands, but Annie was the only one who really needed any control in that respect. Blackjack never broke into a canter; he loved to trot so much, and Frosty rarely wanted to canter.

"Easy, Blackjack. Easy," ordered Heather as she slowed her horse. Blackjack threw his head up. He didn't want to stop.

Nicholas and Laura, seeing that Heather wanted to return to a walk, told their horses to slow down too. All three horses were reluctant, but at last, they obeyed.

"That was awesome!" shouted Nicholas.

"She's amazing! I love her!" exclaimed Laura. "I've got to convince Dad to keep her!"

As the group walked back to the farm, Laura asked Heather if she planned to show Annie. "I don't know," was the answer.

"What about the Spring Morgan Show?" suggested Laura. "We go every year and it's a good show to start the season."

"But I can't show Annie there," protested Heather. "It's a Morgan show and since we don't have Annie's papers, we can't bring her there."

"I thought you knew—"

"Knew what?" asked Heather.

"Last year they added some classes for non-Morgans."

"Non-Morgans? Really?"

"Yeah. There aren't a lot of classes to choose from but I'm pretty sure there's something for Annie. I know there are several dressage classes open to other breeds. I think there are also a couple of pleasure classes and maybe an equitation class. Did Dad get a class list yet?"

"I don't know. We'll have to ask him when we get back. I'd sure love to show Annie."

The ride up to Maine took several hours, but Chauncy didn't mind. Mrs. Campbell had agreed to accompany her husband, provided they stopped at some of the quaint New England shops on the way home. Leaving early in the morning, they arrived at the auction house right before lunch.

After finding the office empty, Chauncy peered down the barn aisle and hollered "Hello there. Anybody around?"

"I'm down here," came the reply.

Chauncy followed the voice to the end of the barn where he found a middle-aged man busy grooming a tall, lanky thoroughbred inside one of the stalls. "I'm Chauncy Campbell. I called you a few weeks ago asking about a Morgan mare who went through one of your sales."

"Oh yeah. Dad said you called again yesterday saying you'd be coming today. Sure, hold on." Giving the horse a friendly pat on the neck, he exited the stall and greeted Chauncy and his wife. "I'm Dan Ventern, otherwise known as Dan Junior. I hate to do this to you, but I'm pretty busy now; we had a load of horses delivered from out west and I've got to prep them for our auction this weekend. But my dad is around here somewhere and he can help you."

Mr. Ventern headed up to the front of the barn and disappeared out the door. As Chauncy and Mrs. Campbell slowly made their way in the same direction, an elderly gentleman popped his head into the barn. "Mr. Campbell? Hi there. I'm Dan Senior but everybody calls me Pops. Sorry I didn't see you drive in; I was out in the field with a horse. Come on up to the office and I'll see what I can do to help."

The Campbells followed Pops into a small, cramped office next to the indoor arena. There was a glass window, apparently so that anyone working in the office could follow the action in the ring. "Right here," said Pops as he pulled out a big black three-ring binder overstuffed with papers. "These are the sales receipts for this year. Do you know what month your mare came through?"

"Actually," corrected Chauncy, "we're pretty sure she sold two years ago."

"Oh," replied the old man.

Chauncy didn't like the sound of that. "Is there a problem?"

"Um . . . not sure. Some of the paperwork may be missing. We hired an office worker a few years back who did a terrible job with record keeping. We fired him after only six months. Unfortunately, that means there are plenty of messed up receipts. Out of order, wrong sale dates, that sort of thing. Here's the binder," said Pops as he grabbed a dusty black binder from another corner of the office. The binder was as overstuffed as the first, but this one had papers that were actually falling out.

"If you have any questions," said Pops, "I'll either be in the barn or out in the field. There's no cell service here so feel free to use the phone as long as the call is local. No long distance calls please."

"Yes, of course," replied Chauncy. "And thank you."

Taking the heavy file, Chauncy sat down on a squeaky chair next to an old wooden desk. Mrs. Campbell pulled up the only other seat in the office, a padded green chair. Its plastic covering was ripped, and the stuffing was falling out. When she sat down, Mrs. Campbell laughed as the chair rocked back and forth on uneven legs. "Only for you and your horses would I put up with this," softly teased Chauncy's wife.

"Let's see," mumbled Chauncy as he opened the binder. "First one . . ." Looking at the receipt, Chauncy had to squint to make out the handwriting. "Quarter Horse gelding. Well, I think we can skip this one." Turning the page, he focused his attention on the next receipt. "Quarter Horse gelding. Hmmm . . . next."

Progress was slow, but after a few hours, the Campbells had picked out four receipts with horses matching Annie's description. "Time to start calling?" asked Chauncy.

"Might as well," agreed Mrs. Campbell.

Each receipt had the name, address, and phone number of the seller and buyer. Deciding to call the buyers first, it was easy to eliminate three horses. Two still owned their horses and the third had sold her Morgan to someone in Wyoming. "Probably not them," concluded Chauncy. "Let's try the last one."

It was impossible to make out the name of the buyer, but after dialing the number, Chauncy was surprised and relieved to hear the voice of the horse trader who had sold Annie to Mrs. Collins. Chauncy recognized his grumpy attitude immediately. Quickly explaining why he was calling, Chauncy hurriedly hung up the phone; he had found the sales receipt for Annie! Checking out the name of the seller, Chauncy was eager to call him. "Looks like Annie's first owner was Mr. Bill Johnson," he excitedly told his wife. "I think we'll have our mystery solved in a few minutes."

As the phone rang, Chauncy held his breath. After three rings, a monotone female voice, a recording, answered, saying "The number you have dialed, 2-5-3-8-8-9-5, has been disconnected. No further information is available. The number you have—"

Chauncy slammed the receiver down. "It's been disconnected. Can you believe it? The guy must have moved."

Carefully removing the receipt from the binder, Chauncy and his wife left the office to find Pops.

"I don't know him," said Pops when asked about Mr. Johnson. "But maybe my son does. Let me ask. Hey Dan, do you remember a Mr. Bill Johnson? These folks think they've found their horse's previous owner but his phone has been disconnected."

"No, don't think so," came a voice from midway down the barn.

"Sorry, Mr. Campbell. We don't have any way of finding the guy other than through these receipts. Maybe—"

"Hold on, Dad," interrupted Dan Junior. Opening the stall door and sticking his head out, he slowly said, "I think I do remember Mr. Johnson. He was Joe Dixon's friend, wasn't he? They sometimes brought horses to the sales together? Yeah, that's him. He moved to Plainville. Why don't you try calling the operator and getting his phone number?"

"Thanks, I'll do that," replied Chauncy as he once again headed to the office. Calling the operator, he immediately got the number for Mr. Bill Johnson and gave the man a call. The phone rang and rang and rang, but there was no answer. "Nobody home," sighed Chauncy.

"That's okay dear. We've got his number. There's no reason why we can't call him from home. We really need to head home if we want to have time to visit some shops and be back by dinner."

With that, the Campbells left the office, thanked Dan Junior and Dan Senior, climbed into the truck and headed back to Gallant Morgans. Chauncy was sure he would soon solve the mystery surrounding Annie.

DISCOVERY AT THE HORSE SHOW

C hauncy returned from Maine in a great mood. The trip had been long but successful; he had found, he hoped, the name of Annie's original owner. When he saw Heather the next day, he immediately updated her on the events, on the name of Annie's first owner, and the likelihood that the mare would soon be registered.

Heather was impatient to learn Annie's true heritage, but she was also excited about the upcoming horse show. When the class list for the show arrived, Heather was thrilled to learn that Laura had been correct when she said that there were a few classes at the Morgan Horse Show that allowed other breeds. There were several dressage classes open to all breeds as well as five other classes. Two of those classes were perfect for Annie, a novice pleasure class open to all breeds and 'First Year Teams,' a class designed for riders who were paired with their current horse for a year or less.

Blackjack would also go to the show. He loved parading in front of the crowds and would get upset if he couldn't attend. Heather entered him in three

Morgan classes: in-hand, pleasure, and his favorite, road hack. It was going to be a fun day!

The Spring Morgan Horse Show was one of the first shows of the year. Horses were still losing their winter coats, and many were out of shape from a long winter of easy living. Owners with no access to indoor arenas, who were forced to practice in still-muddy outdoor rings, were not quite ready to compete. Many stayed home, leading to a low number of entries in some of the classes. Others, who braved the cool spring temperatures, showed horses who were frisky or perhaps still inexperienced in the show ring. For these reasons, the show had a reputation as a low-key event, one that many people used more as a training tool than a place to collect ribbons.

"I wish you brought Rusty," said Heather as Laura drove her dad's pickup truck along the bumpy dirt road into the fairgrounds. "Last time we showed here, he won the trail class and was awesome! I'd love to see him do that again."

"Yeah, that was fun," smiled Laura as she concentrated on driving. "Unfortunately, unless Dad buys a bigger trailer, we're stuck showing two horses at a time."

"Well, you know . . ." started Heather. "Once Annie starts having beautiful babies, somebody will have to show those foals, right?"

"Sure," agreed Laura, knowing how much Heather loved to show.

"We'll need at least a four-horse trailer. Then, with Rusty coming along—"

By the way," said Laura, changing the subject, "is Karen coming?"

"Oh, yeah. Her dad is dropping her off in an hour or so and she's coming home with us."

"She's bringing donuts?"

"Of course," laughed Heather.

Laura pulled into a parking spot next to an enormous eight-horse trailer with a living compartment in the front. "That one! Chauncy should buy that one!" exclaimed Heather.

"Sure, no problem," replied Laura, knowing there was no way her father could afford such an expensive trailer. "You keep dreaming Heather," sighed Laura as both girls climbed out of the vehicle.

It didn't take long to pick up the competition numbers for Blackjack and Annie, get their stall assignments, and see that the horses were comfortably settled in their stalls. Blackjack would be showing first, in his in-hand class. Heather had already spent a lot of time grooming the handsome stallion earlier that morning, but he still needed a quick touch-up. While Laura took care of the horse, Heather disappeared into a third stall they were using as a dressing room.

Heather gathered her hair up into a bun, secured it with pins, wrapped it in a hairnet, and plastered her whole head with hairspray. "Bleck, bleck," she grumbled as she spit hairspray from her mouth.

"You okay in there?" asked Laura, hearing the funny noise.

"Yes. I swallowed hairspray."

"Ew, yuck!"

Heather smiled. Her head felt like cement, but at least every hair would stay in place all day.

"Almost ready?" came Laura's voice several minutes later. "Blackjack's class was called."

"Here I am!" announced Heather as she emerged into the morning sun.

Laura handed the reins of Blackjack's show bridle to her friend. The leather bridle was decorated with a bright red, patent leather band around the horse's forehead and a matching band around his nose. With a small, white half-moon tuft of hair on his forehead, the animal had just enough color to highlight his big, bright eyes. Heather stopped to admire her horse who had put himself into a show stretch. The Morgan arched his neck and gave out a loud whinny. He wanted the world to know he was coming. "Such a show off!" laughed Heather as she gave Blackjack a big pat on his neck and led the animal toward the show ring.

Heather, Laura, and Blackjack patiently waited by the in-gate until their class was called. Looking around, Heather was disappointed to see only three other horses. She loved big classes with lots of competition, but it didn't appear as though that would happen today.

Blackjack stood quietly by Heather's side, and slowly, his eyes began to close as his head drooped. He cocked one back foot to rest it and looked like an old work horse, but when the gate opened and his owner clucked to him, he instantly came to life. He snorted, pranced in place, and when asked, stormed into the ring. Laura followed Heather and Blackjack, holding a long whip off to her side. She would never use the whip on the horse, but rather use it as an extension of her arm, to guide the horse and help keep him on the rail.

Trotting to the far end of the ring, Blackjack was asked to pose in the typical show stretch, front legs together, rear legs slightly back. He stretched out, nostrils flaring, eyes bright, and ears pricked forward. The stallion appeared as if he might explode at any moment. Of course, Heather knew he was simply showing off; he would never do anything dangerous.

Because it was such a small class, it didn't take long for the other horses to enter the ring, pose, and be judged. Blackjack was the last horse to be evaluated, and he waited patiently for the judge, a middle-aged man, dressed neatly in a navy blue business suit and derby hat. He carried a clipboard and pen, and slowly made his way around the black stallion, carefully studying every part of the animal's body. When he finished examining Blackjack, the judge asked Heather to walk the horse to the rail and trot along the fence. The handsome horse energetically trotted down the rail, legs snapping up, head held high, and mane blowing in the breeze.

Reaching the far end of the ring, Heather brought her horse back to a walk. With Laura following behind them, the group made a full circle around the ring, bringing the stallion behind the other horses and back to their starting point. By the time they returned to their spot, the judge had already placed the class. Waiting for the results, Heather was overjoyed to hear the announcer exclaim, "The winner of class 8, Morgan Stallion In-Hand, is number 22, Gallant Image, owned and shown by Heather Richardson."

"All right, Blackjack!" congratulated Laura as she followed the stallion and Heather to the center of the ring to collect their blue ribbon. Once out of the ring, Laura suggested, "We better get back to the stalls immediately. We don't have much time to get Blackjack ready for your pleasure class. I think there are only two classes before you go in."

"Yikes!" replied Heather. "We better hurry."

Back at the stalls, Laura grabbed Blackjack's saddle while Heather added the second bit and set of reins to the horse's bridle. It was always removed when a saddle seat horse was shown in-hand. Heather was in a rush, and Blackjack was anxious to

The handsome horse energetically
trotted down the rail.

get back to the ring and refused to stand still. "Come on, Blackjack! Stop moving around," ordered the frustrated girl. Blackjack shook his head and pawed as the second bit was placed in his mouth. While Heather buckled the leather cheek piece to the bridle, Laura ran a brush through the stallion's tail.

"All set," announced Laura.

"Now stand still!" commanded Heather as she slipped her left foot into the stirrup and swung herself into the saddle. Blackjack pranced in place, unable to contain his excitement.

"I bet he thinks you're going in the road hack class," guessed Laura.

"He's going to be disappointed when we don't get to do a hand gallop!" predicted Heather as she gathered her reins and allowed the horse to trot.

"Heels down!" yelled Laura as the pair disappeared around the corner of the building.

Heading toward the ring, Laura briefly stopped at the food booth to buy a soda. By the time she arrived at the arena, Heather's pleasure class had begun. There were eight horses in the ring, all very nice looking. Most of the animals were well-behaved, and the judge had to watch carefully to find subtle differences between the various horses. He wanted to see a horse with nice collection at all gaits, smooth transitions from the walk to the trot and from the walk to the canter, a nice head-set—no head tossing or fighting with the bits—and a happy, energetic attitude with ears forward. There was so much to remember that Heather sometimes forgot to keep Blackjack collected as she worked on her hand position to keep the stallion happy in the bridle. Other riders, too, had trouble remembering everything which is why friends and trainers along the rail would whisper corrections as riders trotted past.

"Loosen your curb rein," corrected a woman near Laura as a young man on a short, fat, chestnut gelding rode by them.

"How's she doing?"

"Huh? What? Oh, hi Karen!" Laura said as she turned and realized who was standing next to her. "Good! I think it's between her and that rider over there," she explained as she pointed to a teenager in a dark green saddle suit straight across from them.

"Where's Heather?" asked Karen, unable to spot her friend immediately.

"Over there, behind that bay mare."

"Oh, I see her," replied Karen as she watched Heather come out from her hidden spot and make a fantastic pass down the rail. "Wow, they look great!"

Karen and Laura watched the rest of the class in silence. When Heather lined up in center ring, the judge looked her over carefully. Walking down the line of exhibitors, the judge took one last look, scribbled his winners onto a card, and left the ring.

"We have the winners of class 11, Open English Pleasure. The winner is number 25, Megan Lansky and What a Joker."

Heather watched as the teen and her horse trotted to the ringmaster to collect their ribbon. "You were right," observed Karen, "that's the rider you thought had the best chance of winning besides Heather. She's a nice rider—"

"Second place goes to number 22, Heather Richardson and Gallant Image."

Trotting out of the ring, Heather was met by Laura and Karen.

"Congrats!" shouted Karen.

"Thanks!"

"I don't think we have much time," Laura said as she tried to rush her friends back to the barn.

"Again?" groaned Heather as she urged Blackjack into a snappy trot.

Returning to the barn, Laura grabbed the class list. "I was right; we only have a little time to get Annie ready, and I bet you'll want to warm her up a bit too."

Laura, as the groom, brushed Annie while Heather returned Blackjack to his stall and removed his bridle and saddle. She didn't want to risk getting dirt on her fancy saddle suit so she'd leave the brushing to Laura. Turning to exit the stall, Heather heard her horse sigh and drop to the ground. She turned in time to see a horse who had been sparkling clean moments before, rolling in the bedding, clanking his hooves on the wooden side walls as he went back and forth. Heather was sure she saw a smile on Blackjack's face. The girl grinned and left the stall.

"Almost ready," said Laura. "Where's the saddle?"

"Right here," replied Heather, handing it to Laura.

"Can I do anything?" asked Karen.

"Sure! Did you remember to pick up donuts?"

"Oh yeah, forgot about them." Karen went over to a bale of hay next to Blackjack's stall, picked up a small grooming towel that had been thrown onto the hay, and revealed a box of donuts. Tossing her hands into the air, she shouted, "Ta-dah!"

"Oh, I want a chocolate one!" excitedly said Heather.

"Me too! No, wait! How about a jelly?"

The rush of getting ready was disrupted for a brief moment while the three girls gobbled down their donuts. Then it was back to getting Annie ready.

The friends tacked the horse up, and when ready, Laura held Annie while Heather mounted. "Nervous?" asked Laura.

"A little. I'm not sure what she'll do."

"She'll be fine. Relax."

Heather rode Annie toward the ring in a relaxed walk. Arriving at the in-gate, Heather was relieved to see that the class before hers was just starting. She figured they had 10 or 15 minutes before they'd enter the ring. That was plenty of time to warm up the chestnut mare and see how she felt.

Annie, sensing the impending class, began to get nervous. Heather had no way of knowing the mare was having visions of Jim Spencer and his assistant Kevin. She hadn't been to a show since before the fire, since before she'd escaped from the horrible training barn. Annie jigged and tossed her head as they moved along the rail. Breaking into a trot when her rider asked, the horse continued to be tense, but unlike her previous trainers, Heather stayed calm and didn't get angry with the horse. She talked to the Morgan, relaxed her body, and let Annie fidget. The horse, who was used to having the bit snapped back in her mouth when she got nervous at a show, continued to expect pain, but slowly, very slowly, she relaxed a little.

Heather was disappointed but not worried. She didn't know that Annie had been shown and thought the mare was nervous simply because she had never been in a show ring. Bringing the horse back to a walk, Heather stroked the mare's neck and continued to talk. Annie still jigged but she stopped tossing her head.

Heather had entered Annie in the Novice Pleasure class. Only horses who had not yet won three blue ribbons in pleasure classes were eligible to compete. That meant there probably wouldn't be any top-notch competitors in the class. More likely, most of the horses were similar to Annie in their training. Heather didn't care about her competition; her goal was not to win a blue ribbon. Instead she simply wanted Annie to have a good experience.

"Class 19, Novice Pleasure—Open to All Breeds may enter the ring," commanded the unseen voice blaring through the speakers.

Heather took a deep breath and clucked to Annie. The mare obediently followed another horse into the ring. Annie wanted to cling to that other horse as they moved down the rail. Heather didn't fight the mare; she figured Annie was nervous and being near another horse might help.

"They look good," noted Karen as she and Laura found a place on the fence. With arms resting on the top rail, Laura watched carefully. She knew her dad would want a full report. *Annie*, thought Laura, *looks okay*. She had good action at the trot and a nice head-set, but was a bit tense. Like Heather, Laura thought the nervousness was due to this being Annie's debut performance.

The class went quickly as the judge observed each of the nine horses from his vantage point in center ring. Annie went well, picked up her canter without too much trouble, and kept her ears forward most of the time. Her only real problem was that she didn't want to do a flatfooted walk. If Jim Spencer could have seen this horse, who he had forced into the western division, now showing fairly well in saddle seat, he would have thought Heather achieved her magic with cruelty, not love.

Waiting for the judge's decision, Heather adjusted the back of her jacket and then looked over to Laura and smiled. Annie played with her bit while goopy white foam dripped from her mouth. The winner of the class was the young man on the short, fat, chestnut gelding who had competed against Heather in the pleasure class. His horse was a Morgan as were, guessed Heather, one or two others. The rest were a mixture of Arabians, Saddlebreds, and grade horses.

Heather watched patiently as each placing was called. Annie grew restless and didn't want to stand still. As she began to paw, her rider allowed her to walk in a small circle, but upon returning to their spot, Heather insisted the mare stand still. The girl soothed the mare with her calm voice but was interrupted by the announcer, "Taking fifth place is Annie, ridden by Heather Richardson."

"Oh! Good girl! Good girl!" joyfully cheered Heather as she gave Annie a pat and asked the mare to trot over to the ringmaster. The ringmaster congratulated the pair as he placed the pink ribbon on Annie's bridle. The metal backing on the ribbon itched Annie's head, and she shook her head violently. Thinking quickly, Heather leaned forward and removed the ribbon, hung it on her jacket pocket, and left the ring.

"Nice ride," congratulated Laura when they met back at the stalls. Heather had already dismounted and was leading Annie into her stall.

"I'm really pleased with the way she went," said Heather. "It was pretty good for a debut class."

"Dad will be happy," agreed Laura.

"Laura, will you do me a favor?" asked Heather.

"Sure. What?"

"I'm really, really thirsty. That donut made my mouth feel like a desert. Would you mind taking care of Annie so I can get a drink of water?"

"Okay. No problem."

"Thank you so much. I'll meet you at the food booth, okay?"

"Yup, see you soon."

Heather dashed off to the vendor area where hamburgers, hot dogs, drinks, and cookies were sold. She ordered a bottle of water, and while she was there, figured she might as well grab a hamburger too. Waiting for her meal to be cooked, she stood off to the side of the booth and looked around. Spotting a familiar face at one of the nearby tables, Heather waved.

"Heather? Hi!" said a blonde woman as she got up from her table and walked over to Heather.

"Jennifer! I thought that was you. Are you showing?" asked Heather. Jennifer was an old friend of Laura's, a fellow horse lover who had competed against Laura and Rusty for several years.

"Yes, I showed my weanling colt this morning. And I saw Blackjack in his two classes. He looked awesome!"

"Thanks. Blackjack is a big showoff. It's been a good start to the season."

"Who was that chestnut mare you showed in the novice class? Don't tell me you bought another horse."

"Her name is Annie and no, I didn't buy another horse. She belongs to Chauncy."

"Chauncy bought a new horse? That's so cool. But why did you show her in that class instead of the one for Morgans?" asked Jennifer, a bit confused.

"Because she's not a registered Morgan," explained Heather. Pausing for a moment, she continued, "Well, we think she is, but Chauncy doesn't have her papers yet."

"But you could have still shown her in the Morgan division. As long as she's registered, even if Chauncy just bought her and the papers haven't been sent to him yet you could still—"

"You don't understand," interrupted Heather. "We can't show her in Morgan classes because we think she's a Morgan, but we can't find her original owner. Chauncy is still looking for him."

"Miss? Miss?" asked the cook behind the counter. "Here's your hamburger and water."

"Oh, thank you," said Heather as she walked over to the booth and took her food. Opening the water, she took a long, slow gulp. "That feels so much better. Anyway," she continued, turning her attention back to Jennifer, "Chauncy has traced Annie back to a guy in Maine. He's still trying to get in touch with him, but hopefully he'll hear soon."

"Maine? Maine? Are you sure?"

"Yes. Why?"

"I thought she looked familiar. I'm pretty sure I know who she—"

"Who? Who!" interrupted Heather, unable to stand the suspense.

"I'm willing to bet you her name is Hidden Pond Polly. She belonged to a woman named Mrs. Clayburg, a wealthy woman from New York who owned a bunch of horses and kept them all with a trainer. Anyway, Polly supposedly died in a horrible barn fire a few years ago. But there were lots of rumors floating around that the mare actually escaped the fire and wound up at an auction."

"That's impossible," stated Heather. "There's no way it could be Annie. She's had several owners and Chauncy has been able to track them all back to this one guy."

"Well, I bet it is her. She looks like Polly. Mrs. Clayburg advertised her horses a lot, and I remember seeing a bunch of pictures of Polly in the Morgan Horse Magazine. She was a real cute mare. I saw her shown a few times too. Unfortunately, she didn't go as well for Jim Spencer as she went for you today—"

"Jim Spencer?" mumbled Heather. Suddenly Heather felt her stomach twist into knots. Heather knew Jim Spencer to be a horrible man who was a cruel and abusive trainer. He had briefly gotten his hands on Blackjack and terrified the horse. Frosty, too, had fallen victim to his terrible training methods and was now unable to be ridden in a ring, so frightened of her past experiences. Thinking about this, Heather began to realize that there was a good chance Jennifer was correct about Annie. The woman had a great eye for recognizing horses, remembering which animals had been with what trainers, and an encyclopedic talent for knowing the parents and grandparents of many show horses. Plus, Annie reacted much the same way Frosty did when ridden in the ring the first few times, frightened and confused.

"Yeah, she was in training with Jim Spencer. Spencer used to have an assistant trainer named Kevin, and it was Kevin who showed Polly most of the time. I know they showed the mare western and she never did very well. Of course, it wasn't her fault. Something happened to Kevin during the fire—"

"The fire was at Jim Spencer's place?" asked Heather.

"Yeah, and it burned their lower barn to the ground. Fortunately, most of the horses had gone home to their owners for the winter and supposedly only Polly was left in the barn."

"That's horrible," said Heather, feeling ill at the thought.

"And what was it that happened to Kevin?" Jennifer asked herself. "Oh, now I remember. He broke his arm. Claimed it was from trying to rescue Polly, but I bet it was from the horse running over him. He was such a jerk. Heard he quit that job and is now managing a supermarket."

"Gosh, that poor horse," sighed Heather. If Annie was truly Hidden Pond Polly, then she'd probably have to go back to her original owner, and that meant she'd be returned to Jim Spencer for training. How could she allow that to happen to Annie?

"So is Laura here today?" asked Jennifer, changing the subject. "I'd love to see her."

Blurting out an answer before she realized what she was saying, Heather replied, "No, she couldn't get away from school this weekend. My dad took me today. Actually, he's back at the barn waiting for me. We're supposed to be heading home now because he's got some big, important meeting this afternoon. I better hurry up and get going. See ya," said Heather as she dashed off.

Throwing her uneaten hamburger in the trash, Heather hurried back to the barn area. She was incredibly upset. What had she done? She had lied to Jennifer. What a stupid thing to do. Why did she lie? It was to protect Annie, of course. But that didn't make it okay to lie, did it?

Taking a quick gulp from her water bottle, Heather tried to think of something clever to say to Laura. She certainly couldn't tell Laura that Jennifer was at the show. If she did, Laura would insist on tracking her down and spending time together. Then, of course, Jennifer would tell Laura about Annie, and Jim Spencer, and Mrs. Clayburg. That would lead to Annie's being sent back to Mrs. Clayburg and returning to Mr. Spencer's barn. Heather refused to do that to such a sweet mare. She had to protect Annie.

Heather was trying to decide what to say.

"Are you okay, Heather? You don't look very well."

"I don't feel good, Laura. I ate a hamburger and it tasted funny. Maybe it was bad. Can we go home?"

"Are you sure? You still have two classes to go. How about sitting and resting for a little while?"

"No, I really want to go home. Please," pleaded Heather, afraid that Jennifer might walk around the corner at any moment.

"Okay, sure. I'll go scratch your classes, and then Karen and I will get the horses loaded into the trailer. Are you well enough to pack up your saddle suit?"

"Yeah. I can do it. I just want to go home." And with that, Heather had created an even bigger lie. She felt fine. She desperately wanted to show Blackjack and Annie, but she wanted to protect Annie far more than show. It was okay, she decided, to lie if it meant saving an innocent horse from a terrible fate.

A Growing Lie

Heather didn't go to the barn for a few days. She had told Laura she felt sick at the horse show and repeated the lie when she saw Chauncy at the barn. How could she simply show up the next day as if nothing were wrong? She pretended to have a stomach bug and even stayed home from school for a day.

Finally, almost a week after the horse show, Heather got the nerve to visit her horses. She hoped she wouldn't run into Chauncy, but as soon as she entered the barn, there he was, sweeping the aisle. Karen was there too.

"Hi," said Heather, walking quietly over to Blackjack's stall.

"Heather! Are you all better?" asked Karen.

"Yeah. I feel much better."

"I figured you must have been pretty sick," added Chauncy. "It takes a lot to keep you away from your horses."

Heather weakly smiled and tried to get away from her friends. "Oh, Heather! Guess what? Guess what?" questioned Karen.

"What?" asked Heather, pretending to be interested in Karen's surprise.

"Rerun is getting better! Come look!" Heather followed Karen to Rerun's stall. "See?" continued Karen as she showed her Miniature Horse's clipped back to Heather. "The bump is getting smaller! I've continued to apply the medication and look; the bump has finally started to go away!"

"Wow, Karen," replied Heather, now slightly interested in what was going on. "That's really great. Hopefully the bump will go completely away."

"I hope so," agreed Karen. Leaving the stall for a moment, she grabbed Rerun's halter from the front of the stall door and slipped it onto the horse. Heather watched as Karen led her little friend to the cross ties at the front of the barn and began grooming the mare.

Deciding that she didn't really feel like riding, Heather groomed Blackjack, then Rusty, Frosty, Annie, and finally Shadow, all in their stalls. She was lost in silent thought, brushing the knots out of Shadow's tail, when Chauncy walked up, "Are you okay?"

"Yeah, sure. Why do you ask?" said Heather, startled that Chauncy would think anything was wrong.

"You seem quiet today. Is something bothering you?"

"No, I'm okay. Really I am, Chauncy." Seeing the look in Chauncy's eyes, Heather was sure her friend was not convinced. "I guess I'm still a little under the weather from the stomach bug." Watching Chauncy walk away, Heather was amazed how he was able to pick up on her unusual behavior so easily. Returning her attention to Shadow, Heather tried to forget that she had lied to Chauncy, something she had never done.

"Oh, Heather," said Chauncy, returning to Shadow's stall. "I forgot to tell you, I finally heard from Bill Johnson."

"Who?"

"Bill Johnson, the man who sold Annie to the horse trader in Maine. Remember?"

"Oh, him," said Heather, as if in a daze.

"Are you sure you're okay?" asked Chauncy again.

"Yes, really, I'm fine Chauncy." Heather suddenly realized that if Mr. Johnson was Annie's original owner, then Jennifer was wrong about the mare's past. This could be the information they needed to keep Annie. "You found Annie's first owner?" she asked, swiftly coming to life.

"Well, the good news is that yes, I did manage to track down Bill Johnson. The bad news is that it appears he isn't Annie's first owner. Turns out he found her running along his fence early one morning. Can you believe it? Annie appeared out of the mist, whinnying and trying to get into his pasture. Sounds like a movie, doesn't it?" smiled Chauncy.

"Then where did she come from?" mumbled Heather, dropping her brush into the shavings. Shadow, always wanting to chew on anything she could find, grabbed the brush and started playing with it. Heather ignored her filly as she tried to think of a way to keep Chauncy from finding out the truth about Annie. If he discovered her identity, he'd probably send the sweet mare back to Jim Spencer's place. How could she let that happen? She had to do whatever was necessary to protect Annie.

"Mr. Johnson doesn't know. He says there was a barn fire about 20 miles from his place the day before Annie showed up and suspects that she may have escaped from that farm. But when he called the place, they said they weren't missing any horses. Still, nobody else had a missing horse. He looked for a week or so before sending her off to auction."

"What are you going to do?" asked Heather. Was this the end of the search for Annie's secret past? Would Chauncy sell her now? *He couldn't*, thought Heather. She was a Morgan, papers or not, and she was too sweet to sell. Heather felt herself getting sick to her stomach, this time for real.

"I'm not sure," admitted Chauncy. "I've got to think about it for a bit. I can't spend much more time trying to get her registration papers. I'll probably make a few phone calls and see if anybody is interested in buying her."

"You can't do that!" exclaimed the girl.

"I know you're attached to her, Heather, but remember, I told you I might have to sell Annie."

"But she is a registered Morgan!" blurted out Heather.

Looking puzzled, Chauncy asked, "Do you know something that I don't, Heather?"

Realizing she had almost exposed Annie's secret, Heather tried to cover up her mistake. "No, Chauncy, I don't know anything. But I'm sure she's a purebred, and I know if you wait, we'll find her original owner."

Chauncy smiled uneasily. He sensed Heather was hiding something, but he didn't know what. "We'll see," he concluded, as he walked away.

Riding home in the car with her mom, Heather said very little. This was probably the first time she had not enjoyed her time at the barn. She was afraid to talk to anyone, even her mother, fearing she might expose Annie's secret.

Heather still held out hope that Jennifer was wrong, that Annie was not Hidden Pond Polly. She was Annie Bananie, a sweet, wonderful Morgan mare, who once belonged to a little girl in New Hampshire. At least that was what Heather wanted to believe.

"Oh, Heather, there's a letter for you on the counter," said Mrs. Richardson as the pair walked into their house.

Curious to see who was sending her mail, Heather immediately opened the letter. Realizing quickly that it was from Jennifer, Heather read the note rapidly.

"Who is it from?" asked Mrs. Richardson, interrupting Heather's thoughts.

"Nobody, Mom. Just a horse friend," muttered Heather as she disappeared into her room. The note was short and simply said that Jennifer had found an old ad for Hidden Pond Polly and was sending it along so Heather could see the uncanny resemblance the mare had to Annie. Nervously turning the page, Heather was astonished to see a picture of Annie, in a show stretch at some show the girl didn't recognize. The text under the ad read, 'Introducing Our Newest Show Ring Star, Hidden Pond Polly.' At the bottom corner of the page appeared the notation, 'In Training With Jim Spencer.' But it wasn't the writing that caught Heather's attention. It was the horse's eyes. Staring into those big, sweet eyes, Heather saw Annie staring back at her. Annie was Hidden Pond Polly. Crinkling up both papers, Heather tossed them into her wastebasket. She wasn't going to tell anybody.

THE JUSTIN
MORGAN CLASS

It was the morning of the Vermont Country Morgan Show, and Heather arrived at the farm before the sun was up. She was tired and grumpy and didn't feel like traveling all the way to Vermont.

Yawning as she silently walked into the barn, her eyes adjusted to the dim lights in the building. "Hi, Chauncy," she casually said as she saw Chauncy searching for something in the tack room.

"Oh, hi there, Heather!" said an enthusiastic Chauncy. *At least he's excited*, thought Heather. "All set for today?"

"Yeah, I guess so," she replied, entering Blackjack's stall to groom him. As she quietly worked on her stallion, Heather's mind began to wander to thoughts of Annie. The mare was in a nearby stall, happily eating her hay. Chauncy hadn't mentioned anything about his quest to find her first owner in a few weeks so maybe he'd given up. Would he keep her now?

Heather stopped brushing Blackjack as she became lost in thought. She didn't want to go to the show today because she was worried about Annie.

How could she have fun with Blackjack when she was so concerned about another horse? Thinking about what might happen to Annie if she were returned to Jim Spencer, Heather realized she hadn't enjoyed coming to the farm since the day she had learned Annie's true identity. Worrying about a special horse sure took the fun out of everything.

Suddenly Heather was pushed violently forward. "Hey! Cut that out!" she yelled at Blackjack, who had shoved her with his nose. Looking into the handsome stallion's big, sweet eyes, she understood that he simply wanted her full attention. "I'm sorry, buddy. I didn't mean to snap at you," Heather said, feeling bad for the way she had scolded her horse. Blackjack snorted, gently nuzzled the girl, and then sneezed on her. "Ew, yuck!" said Heather in a playful manner as she returned to brushing the Morgan.

As daylight began to creep through the barn, Heather loaded Blackjack on the trailer. Chauncy had put the racing sulky as well as tack, feed, buckets, and all sorts of other items they might need into the truck bed the night before. Walking out of the trailer, Heather was about to lift the back ramp when Chauncy stopped her. "Wait a minute. I'm bringing Annie along."

"Annie? Why?" asked a surprised Heather.

"There's somebody in Vermont, who lives way up by the Canadian border, interested in Annie. He's looking for a horse for his daughter. Since he lives so far away, I suggested we meet at the show. It'll save him a lot of driving."

"But, Chauncy! You can't sell Annie!" pleaded Heather.

"I don't want to," admitted Chauncy, "but it doesn't look like I'll ever be able to get her papers."

"But she's a Morgan!"

"We think she's a Morgan," corrected Chauncy.

"No, Chauncy. She is a Morgan."

"Heather, is there something you're not telling me?" asked Chauncy. He had sensed there was a problem ever since Heather returned from the Spring Morgan Show.

"No. Why do you ask?"

"Because you seem," Chauncy paused, looking for the right words, "you seem distracted lately."

Heather had to think of something to say fast. She needed to save Annie, to prevent her from getting on that trailer. "I ran into Jennifer McElroy at the show—"

"Jennifer Mc Who?" interrupted Chauncy.

"McElroy. She's a friend of Laura; they used to show against each other."

"Oh, that Jennifer. I remember her."

"Anyway," continued Heather, "she recognized Annie."

"Why didn't you tell me?" asked a surprised Chauncy.

"I'm sorry, Chauncy. I didn't want to tell you until I knew for sure, in case Jennifer was wrong. She's pretty sure Annie is from New Jersey, that she was a trail horse—"

"How on earth would Jennifer know a horse who was used for trail riding?" interrupted Chauncy again. "And how did a horse go from living in New Jersey to running loose through a field in Maine?"

Heather was getting caught in her own lie. Chauncy was right. How would Jennifer, living in New Hampshire, know about a trail horse so far away? Quick, say something fast. "Um, Jennifer used to trail ride with the girl who owned Annie. They lost track of each other, but Jennifer is trying to locate her for us. She remembers hearing that her friend from New Jersey went on an overnight ride in Maine and the horse got loose. A whole bunch of people looked for the horse, but they never found the mare. I didn't want to tell you until I knew for sure."

Chauncy wasn't sure what to believe. The story didn't sound right to him, but still, Heather had never lied before.

"Where are you going?" asked Heather, seeing that Chauncy was going into the barn.

"I told the gentleman from northern Vermont that I would bring Annie for him to see, and I intend to honor my promise."

Her story hadn't worked! How could that be? "But Chauncy! Annie is a Morgan. We'll have her papers soon."

"I'm sorry, Heather, but I'm taking Annie to Vermont."

Deciding there wasn't much she could do, Heather climbed into the back seat of the truck. Karen and Nicholas arrived a moment later, dropped off by Karen's dad. "Hi Heather!" said Karen as she got into the truck.

"Hey," said Nicholas, following Karen's lead.

"Hi guys," replied Heather, trying to hide her anxiety. "What's up?"

Karen started talking a mile a minute about the Justin Morgan class. She asked all sorts of questions and simply couldn't wait to watch Blackjack race down a track. Heather did her best to patiently answer every question while Nicholas yawned, slouched back in the seat, and closed his eyes. Hearing a thump, thump, thump, coming from the trailer, Heather knew Annie was loaded. Maybe she wouldn't come home. What a horrible thought.

"All set?" asked Chauncy as he got into the truck. Beeping the horn twice, he stared at his house until a minute later his wife appeared. Dressed in a pretty skirt and jacket, she was carrying a bag full of goodies. *Drinks and snacks for the road*, thought Heather. Mrs. Campbell didn't normally come to horse shows, but the Justin Morgan class was a special event, and she loved watching her husband compete.

"Here I am!" said Mrs. Campbell as she handed Chauncy her bag while she lifted herself up into the truck.

Karen was still talking non-stop about Robin and their last trail ride when the horse had been so lazy that she lowered her head until she actually tripped over her nose, the fact that Rerun's bump was almost gone, and how late they'd all get home after today's show. "It'll be so cool," she exclaimed. "My mom will be fast asleep before I get back to the house. Dad wasn't very thrilled about how late he'd have to pick me up."

Nicholas smiled while Heather did her best to join in the conversation. She didn't want her friends to know how upset she was at the thought of Annie leaving. Although Karen liked Annie, she never spent any time with the chestnut mare; all her affection went to Robin and Rerun. Unlike Heather, Karen had taken Chauncy's advice when Annie first arrived and hadn't gotten attached to the mare. She didn't realize that Heather had ignored Chauncy's warning and fallen deeply in love with Annie.

For Heather, the long ride to the show grounds dragged on. At last, after what seemed like hours, the truck slowed down and took a left turn onto a bumpy side road that went steeply down a hill. At the bottom was a wide open field where many trucks and trailers were parked next to several long barns. There was an old racing track at the far end of the field with two riding rings set in the center of the oval. Rickety old bleachers sat along one side of the track, near the finish line.

Chauncy quickly found a parking spot and then had the group wait in the truck while he went to the show office to pick up Blackjack's number and stall assignment. Returning a few minutes later, he asked, "Heather, would you unload Blackjack and Annie? Our stalls are in that end barn over there," as he pointed to the furthest building.

"Okay, Chauncy," replied Heather, in her cheeriest voice. "We'll get the horses settled into their stalls. Karen? Nicholas? Will you help me?"

There was plenty of time to relax before Heather had to get Blackjack ready for the Justin Morgan class. The event was scheduled right before the lunch break, and because they had arrived at the start of the morning session, the group from Gallant Morgans headed to the ring to watch several classes.

Heather leaned against the rail as eight adorable yearling Morgans trotted into the ring being led by people of all ages, some dressed casually in slacks and others outfitted in show attire. One horse caught Heather's attention because it looked just like Shadow. Turning to tell Chauncy how similar she thought the filly was to her horse, she realized he had disappeared. Looking around, she was startled to see him standing near the barn, holding Annie. There was a middle-aged gentleman talking to Chauncy and a young girl in pigtails stroking the mare's neck.

Suddenly Heather felt sick to her stomach—again. This feeling was happening far too often.

Staring at Chauncy, Heather was upset to see him smiling broadly and shaking his head up and down. Was he agreeing to sell Annie? Were these people going to take Annie today? What could she do?

As Heather continued to watch, Chauncy noticed her. Saying something to the man who wanted to buy Annie, Chauncy motioned Heather to come join them. Reluctantly, she excused herself from the gang watching the show and headed over to the barn.

"What's up Chauncy?" she asked hesitantly when she arrived.

"Heather, I'd like you to meet Mr. Maxwell and his daughter Michaela. They're interested in Annie and would like to see her ridden. Would you grab her saddle from the barn and tack her up? You can show them what a nice mare we have for sale."

Heather couldn't believe what she was hearing. Not only was Chauncy selling Annie, but he was asking her to ride the sweet mare. How could he expect her to ride Annie in front of these people? She desperately wanted to say something, to scream, to run away, to do anything but ride Annie. Feeling trapped, she halfheartedly went to the barn, found Annie's tack, and returned to the spot where the mare waited.

Once Heather had readied the Morgan, she mounted and started walking along the edge of the field. "Warm her up a little and then have her trot, Heather. I'd like Mr. Maxwell to see what a great trot she has."

Heather didn't say anything; she simply did as told. After several minutes of walking around a small area at the far end of the field, Heather was about to ask for a trot when she glanced over to the ring. Seeing her friends still happily watching the show, she was shocked to see a familiar face just a few feet away from them. She knew that nasty scowl, the brown hair with gray patches around the temples, the weathered look, and especially the whip. It was Jim Spencer! What was he doing here?

Without realizing it, Heather's whole body tightened just as she was asking for the trot. In response, Annie threw her head up into the air, mouth gaping, ears flat back. Heather immediately turned her attention back to the mare, but, being incredibly upset at the sight of Mr. Spencer, she was unable to relax. Her hands pulled back as her feet flopped about in the stirrup irons. As Annie reacted, Heather's legs instinctively clenched to the mare's side and her heels dug in to the horse's hide.

Startled by her rider's unusual behavior, Annie flung herself forward. Mr. Maxwell didn't seem very impressed by the mare's poor performance, thinking it was all the horse's fault. Michaela didn't understand what the horse was doing, only that Annie was pretty. "Her legs go up really high, Daddy," she told her father.

"Yes, honey, they do. Mr. Campbell? I think I've got a good idea of your mare's talent. She may be too much horse for my daughter; I'm not sure. Anyway, we've got a couple of other horses to look at today before we make a decision. I'll be in touch." Mr. Maxwell shook Chauncy's hand. "Come on, honey. Let's go see some other horses."

As Mr. Maxwell disappeared behind several trucks, Heather managed to regain her composure. Adjusting her body, she brought Annie's head back in, collected the horse's body, and within moments had the mare looking like a sharp little show horse. But it was too late to impress Mr. Maxwell; he was gone.

Chauncy stood by himself. Heather slowed Annie to a walk and approached her mentor. "That was quick. They didn't even watch her go."

Chauncy, not understanding why Heather had ridden so poorly, thought his friend was trying to sabotage the sale. "What was that all about?" he asked, not amused.

"What?"

"The way you rode Annie?"

"You mean when I slipped? I'm sorry, I wasn't paying attention."

"Heather, I've never known you to be caught off guard when riding. Were you trying to lose a sale for me?"

"No!" blurted out Heather. "No, Chauncy, no!" Heather felt herself filling up with tears. "I'm sorry. I didn't mean to mess up my ride, really. I looked over at Nicholas and Karen for a second and lost my balance. It was stupid, and I'm sorry."

"Heather, you need to understand," said Chauncy, changing his voice to a gentler tone. "I can't get Annie's papers so I have to sell her. I refuse to take her to an auction; she has to go to a good home. So you've got to work with me on this, okay? Together we can find Annie a great home, but you've got to do your part."

"Okay, Chauncy. I promise," meekly agreed Heather as she slid out of the saddle.

Once Annie was back in her stall, Heather kissed her on the nose, latched the stall shut, and dashed outside. Running behind the barn, she sat down in a patch of tall grass, hidden from view. With her knees to her chest, she wrapped her arms around her legs and without warning, burst into tears. It wasn't fair! It just wasn't fair!

After a few moments of crying, Heather realized somebody might hear her. Trying to hold her emotions inside, Heather gasped and sobbed. She slowly regained her composure, wiped away the tears, and stood up. She was relieved to find that she was alone. Taking several deep breaths, she returned to the show.

"Clear the track, please! Clear the track!" boomed the voice over the speakers. "The Justin Morgan harness race will begin in ten minutes."

Nicholas and Karen rushed back to the barn to see Chauncy decked out in a bright yellow and maroon silk racing shirt with matching cap and goggles. Blackjack was hitched to his two-wheeled racing sulky, chomping at the bit. Heather held her stallion tightly as Chauncy climbed into the cart and picked up the horse's reins.

"Awesome!" exclaimed Karen. "Blackjack looks so cool!"

Heather smiled. She was feeling a little better now, because she was concentrating on Blackjack's big race. "He's ready!" she told Chauncy. "Are you all set?"

"Yup, let him go," he told Heather.

Clucking to the bold stallion, Chauncy guided the horse toward the track. Heather, Nicholas, Karen, and Mrs. Campbell, who had been silently watching her husband from the barn, followed.

There were four other driving horses on the track, each warming up by slowly trotting back and forth near the bleachers. As Chauncy entered, an elderly gentleman with a slight limp closed the gate. "All horses are on the track," shouted the announcer. "The race will start in five minutes."

The sparse ringside crowd of the morning had grown into a mob. The bleachers were full, as was much of the space around the track. Blackjack looked incredible; he knew something exciting was about to happen, and he trotted like a park horse, with knees almost hitting his chin, to show his approval. Tossing his head and pulling at the bit, he pleaded with his driver to go fast. Chauncy had to work hard to keep the stallion under control.

"We're ready to start!" yelled the voice over the speakers. "All drivers please take your positions next to the pole horse."

The drivers had drawn numbers out of a hat earlier in the day to determine their starting positions. The man who drew the first position was closest to the inside rail of the track and his horse was called the pole horse. This horse was the first one to trot, moving along the rail. The other racers then guided their horses alongside the pole horse, headed toward a thick white line in the dirt. The pole horse had to be slightly ahead of the others as they passed the line for the race to start.

The track looked like a jumbled mess for a moment as the drivers found their places. Once the horses were in position, they slowly trotted but were obviously impatient to run as they all strained at their bits. Chauncy was in the middle of the pack. Suddenly, a bay horse next to Chauncy broke free of the line and flew forward. "Number 8, please return your horse to the line," ordered the unseen voice.

The driver of the disobedient horse pulled back hard on the reins and waited for the others to catch up. The horse was not happy and he looked like he might dash off again. But at that instant, the pole horse trotted over the white line and the announcer yelled, "It's a race!"

The horses exploded. Two of them broke into a canter immediately and were pulled back by their drivers. The other three burst into a fast trot, with Blackjack and the bay horse next to him taking the lead. "Go! Go! Go!" screamed the group from Gallant Morgans. Heather forgot her earlier problems as she was lost in the excitement of the race. All three kids jumped up and down as they cheered, clapped, and yelled encouragement to Blackjack. Mrs. Campbell, also caught up in the energy of the moment, cheered and clapped.

Blackjack and the bay horse were soon well ahead of the other competitors. The two horses were nose to nose, and it was hard for Heather to see who was leading as they rounded the first corner. "Go, Blackjack, go!" she continued to scream.

Coming out of the first turn, Blackjack was on the outside and with more ground to cover, fell behind the other horse. "No! No! No!" yelled Karen. "Run!"

*Blackjack's legs were a blur of motion
as he caught up to and slowly overtook
the other horse.*

Going down the backstretch, Blackjack's amazing road trot took over. His legs were a blur of motion as he caught up to and slowly overtook the other horse. "Yeah!" hollered Nicholas as he jumped in place.

Turning the last corner, Blackjack was going so fast that Chauncy had to tilt his upper body toward the inner rail to maintain his balance. The cart whizzed around the turn and headed to the finish line. In a flash they flew across the white line to the cheers of the crowd. The bay horse finished several strides behind Blackjack, while the other three horses were much further back.

"We won! We won!" squealed Karen.

Diving under the railing and rushing onto the track, supporters of each horse hurried to their favorite equines. Heather was the first one to reach Blackjack. The handsome stallion wanted to continue the race, but Chauncy insisted he slow to a walk. Heather grabbed the horse's reins and talked to him in a quiet, soothing voice.

Chauncy had an enormous smile on his face as he removed his racing goggles. "How was that?" he asked, obviously quite pleased with himself and Blackjack. "Whoo-boy, that was fun! Heather?"

"Yes, Chauncy?"

"Let's get Blackjack cooled out and then head straight to the barn to change tack. We've only got twenty minutes before your race under saddle."

Justin Morgan's reputation for being able to race, show, and pull weight all on the same day amazed Heather. Blackjack was in great physical shape, and although he was a bit out of breath, he hadn't worked up much of a sweat. Still, she was sure he'd be exhausted by the end of this class.

Back at the barn, Nicholas and Karen helped unhook Blackjack from the cart while Chauncy slipped off his racing silks and gave them to Heather. The jacket was obviously too big for her, with the sleeves bunching around the wrists. "You look like a real jockey," said Karen.

"I feel sort of silly," replied Heather as she put her helmet on. Then she put the goggles on and adjusted the strap so they wouldn't fall off during the race.

Heather helped Nicholas remove the harness from Blackjack, keeping the bridle on until every-thing else was off. Then, wrapping the reins of her riding bridle around Blackjack's neck, she took off the harness bridle with its long, cumbersome reins and quickly put her simple riding bridle on the horse. Meanwhile, Karen put Blackjack's saddle on the stallion, tightening the girth as best she could. "Let me check it," offered Heather as she tightened the girth another notch. "All set, boy?" she asked Blackjack as she mounted.

"Walk him around until they call us," suggested Chauncy.

As Heather and Blackjack made their way to the track, the announcer gave a five-minute warning for the start of the second phase of the class. Walking onto the turf, Heather felt an overwhelming sense of awe. She was about to race her stallion in a class that was modeled after the exploits of Justin Morgan. What an honor that was!

"Are you ready, Blackjack?" asked Heather as she reached forward and stroked her horse's neck. She felt a tinge of excitement run through her body.

"Be careful, okay?" asked Chauncy, patting Heather's lower leg for good luck. "You haven't run him at a full gallop against other horses very often, and I don't want you to lose control."

"I've raced him against Spot and Rusty on trail rides," countered Heather.

"But he wasn't on a track being urged on by other really fast horses," said Chauncy.

"We'll be okay, don't worry."

"Get your horses to the starting line," demanded the voice from the speakers.

Heather guided Blackjack to the familiar white line. Unlike the harness race, this race would start from a standstill, no trotting to the line first. As she waited for the starting bell, she bent forward and grasped a thick mass of Blackjack's mane. Chauncy had warned her that without that, she might lose her balance as the stallion bounded forward. She knew galloping wasn't Blackjack's best talent. In fact, he was kind of slow, so it was really important that they get a good start when the bell rang.

Glancing over to her friends on the rail, Heather smiled. Looking off to the bleachers, she gasped as she noticed Jim Spencer leaning on the rail, staring right at her! What did he—

Suddenly the loud sound of the bell rang through Heather's head. Blackjack jumped in anticipation without waiting for a command to start, but because Heather wasn't paying attention, her hands were clamped tightly and back instead of forward to allow the horse's head to move. Unable to jump ahead, Blackjack instead went up, front feet flying in the air. He landed with a hard thud. Even with the stallion's mane hair clenched in her fist, the young rider lost her balance. Pulling at the reins to steady herself, Heather forced the Morgan's head high against his chest, but his head needed to be out, not in, if he was to gain speed.

Heather's heart raced as she realized her mistake. She was terrified of what Chauncy might say, of what Jim Spencer wanted. Her body started to shake with fear, but Blackjack ignored her tremors as he tried his best to burst from the starting point.

Regaining her balance, Heather kicked her horse and yelled at him to run. The horse obeyed, but by now it was too late. The other four horses all had had good starts and were well ahead of Blackjack and Heather.

Within seconds, Blackjack was at a full gallop. His ears were pinned against his neck. Heather leaned down and forward, just like the jockeys she'd watched on television. The Morgan's long mane blew into her face as they charged onward.

Rounding the last turn, Blackjack managed to catch up to one of the other horses, but there were still three Morgans well in front of them. Try as he might, Blackjack couldn't catch up; the race was lost. As the pair flew across the finish line, Blackjack was a stride behind the other horse; they had finished in last place.

Blackjack didn't want to stop racing. He apparently thought he could still pass the other horses. They easily slowed to a walk while Blackjack continued to run. Heather had to pull back hard to convince the stallion to stop; in fact, they were turning the first corner before the stallion finally broke down to a trot.

Returning to the bleacher area, Blackjack was breathing heavily. Heather jumped down from the saddle, looking around for Jim Spencer. Where had he gone?

"Was that scary?" asked Karen as she rushed to Heather's side.

"A little, yeah." Then Heather spotted Chauncy. Would he yell at her?

"It looked like Blackjack was too much horse for you," observed Chauncy. He didn't seem angry. "Nicholas? Would you take Blackjack and cool him off while Heather changes into her show outfit? We don't have much time."

"Sure, Chauncy," agreed Nicholas as he took the reins from Heather.

Left on her own to get ready, Heather headed in the direction of the barn. Looking at the crowds around the track, Heather stopped suddenly. There in front of her, a few feet away, stood Jim Spencer. He was holding a bay horse; the one who had placed fourth in the galloping race, just in front of Blackjack. A slim young man was sitting on the horse, relaxing as he talked to Jim Spencer. The horse hung its head low and panted.

Staring at the trainer, Heather didn't know what to do. He had to have seen her. And then he looked directly at her and snickered. "Not having a good show with your nag, huh?"

Heather was angered and frightened. She hadn't heard that horrible man's voice since the day she rescued Blackjack from his cruel hands. The sound of it sent shivers down her spine. She veered away from him without saying a word and ran to the barn.

With her show coat on, Heather rushed out of the stall and ran back toward the track. Meeting her halfway was Nicholas, holding Blackjack. Somebody had already put the full bridle on the Morgan, and he was ready to go. Heather mounted her horse and took the reins from Nicholas as he wished her luck.

Then the girl clucked to Blackjack, and the pair headed to one of the rings.

The crowd had moved from the bleachers to the ring in anticipation of both the pleasure class and the stone boat pull. Heather could see two of the competitors already waiting by the gate, and by the time she arrived, the other entrants had arrived.

"Ladies and gentleman," came the familiar voice from the speakers, "we are now ready to start the third section of our Justin Morgan event, the pleasure class. Please open the gate and let the riders enter."

The same elderly gentleman with the slight limp who had manned the racetrack gate was also in charge of the ring gate, and he shooed onlookers away as he carefully opened it. He then motioned to the competitors to enter the ring.

Calling the class to order, the announcer asked for a trot. All the horses were already trotting, having entered the ring in a snappy, high-stepping fashion, but the call meant the judge was now officially watching and deciding his placings.

Heather felt exhausted. She had gotten up early in the morning, sat in a truck for hours, stood out in the sun watching the show, ridden Annie for a stranger and his daughter, had a good cry, and raced Blackjack at a full gallop. Annie. What about Annie?

"Canter, please. All canter."

Again Heather was caught off guard. Another horse had wandered too close to Blackjack. Without his rider's guidance, the stallion, hearing the command, decided to canter immediately. Right into the other horse.

"What's wrong with Heather?" asked Nicholas. "She's not riding very well."

"I don't know," replied Chauncy. He was now certain that something was going on with Heather, and he intended to find out as soon as the Justin Morgan class was over.

Heather, seeing her mistake, immediately corrected her horse by bringing him back to the walk and asking for the canter again. Unfortunately, the judge saw the whole incident and scribbled something on his clipboard.

After a brief canter, the horses were asked to walk and then reverse. Heather thought her horse was tired, but as soon as the trot was called, he happily broke into a brisk, snappy gait. Where was his stamina coming from, she wondered? The power underneath her felt amazing until the stallion had a sudden surge of energy as he approached a bay stallion directly in front of him. Briefly looking at the horse, Heather saw a familiar man standing near the rail, once again staring at her. Why was Mr. Spencer doing this to her? Her legs felt weak and Blackjack must have picked up on her distraction because he used that lapse in riding skill to press forward and pass the other stallion. But as he did so, he broke into a canter, a major fault in a pleasure class.

With only five horses in the ring, it was easy for the judge to see most, if not all, of the errors made. He again saw Heather's mistake and marked it on his paper.

"Blackjack! Stop it!" ordered Heather. She knew it was her error but thought that maybe if she scolded her horse he would behave.

The black stallion was a perfect gentleman for the remainder of the class, picking up his canter easily, with ears pricked forward, nose tucked in at the correct angle, and showing a bright, happy attitude. Was it too late to pin well?

Determined to make a final, good impression on the judge, Heather trotted her horse down the rail as riders were asked to line up in the center of the ring. The judge watched her carefully, again writing something on his pad.

Finding a spot at the end of the line, Heather posed her stallion in the standard show stretch. Blackjack acted as if the whole world were watching him and he loved it. He gave out a loud, deep whinny, shook his head a few times, and looked around. Heather gave him a quick pat as the judge made his way through the line. Making a few more notes on his pad, he then handed it to the ringmaster and left.

"We have the results of the third section of our Justin Morgan class," announced the voice from the speakers a few moments later. "First place goes to Beaming Bright, owned and ridden by Henry

Piker." Several people clapped. Heather looked to her right to see the bay stallion who Blackjack had almost run into trot to the ringmaster to receive his blue ribbon. "Second place is awarded to Class Act, owned by Helen Dixon and ridden by Gary Dixon." More clapping as a pretty chestnut mare received her red ribbon. "Third place goes to Gallant Image, owned and ridden by Heather Richardson."

Heather gave Blackjack a friendly pat as she walked him to the center and collected her ribbon. Exiting the ring, Heather immediately saw Chauncy waiting right by the gate. He gently took hold of Blackjack's bridle and led him to a nearby spot where the horse's work harness was waiting. "Now it's our turn," he told Heather in a kindly manner.

Heather silently removed Blackjack's saddle and then, with Chauncy's help, replaced his riding bridle with the heavier harness bridle. Draping the long reins over the horse's back, she asked Chauncy what else she could do. "I think I'm all set," he replied. "I guess you can join the rest of the group on the rail until the class is called."

Heather quickly found Nicholas, Karen, and Mrs. Campbell and was instantly congratulated by Karen. "Nice ride, Heather."

"Thanks," said Heather. "Although I think I could have done better."

Easing her way in between Karen and Nicholas, Heather rested her arms on the top rail and plopped her head down on her arms. Nicholas leaned over and quietly whispered to Heather, "What's going on? What's bothering you?"

"What?" answered Heather. She didn't realize her mood was so obvious. "What do you mean?"

"Come on Heather. I'm one of your best friends," said Nicholas as he adjusted his glasses. "I can tell when something is wrong."

Deciding it would be pointless to say she was fine, but not willing to admit she knew about Annie's past, Heather told Nicholas only a portion of what was going on. "Jim Spencer is here."

"Jim who?" asked Nicholas.

"Jim Spencer. I told you about him. He's the nasty guy who messed up Blackjack and destroyed any chance of getting Frosty into the show ring."

"Oh, him. What's he doing here?"

"He's a trainer, or at least that's what he thinks. I'm pretty sure one of the bay horses in this class is his."

"You can't let him get to you, Heather."

"I know. I know it's stupid but I can't help it. Do you think Chauncy is mad?"

"No, but I believe he's disappointed. He's been looking forward to this show for a long time, and I think he expected Blackjack to do better in the galloping race and in your ring class. You need to explain what's going on to him so he'll understand."

"As soon as this class is over . . ."

THE CONFESSION

"Five minutes until the stone boat pull. All entrants in the ring please," came the order.

Heather slipped between the fence rails and joined Chauncy in the ring. She was used to seeing Blackjack in his fancy show harness, with thin leather straps designed to allow the animal's shoulders to move freely so the legs could go up with a minimum of interference, but today, all the horses in the ring looked like they were ready to go plow a field. They wore heavy neck collars, thick pieces of leather around the rumps, and bridles with plain leather browbands.

Each horse had two handlers, one who was holding the reins and the other who stood by the horse's head to steady the animal while it was hooked to the stone boat. The stone boat was a simple piece of wood, curved up slightly in the front with a hook for the harness attachment. It was stacked tall with ten 50-pound bags of horse feed, for a total of 500 pounds. The grain, donated by a local feed store, would be taken home by the winner of the Justin Morgan class. At the far end of the ring, a tractor was waiting. After each horse pulled the stone boat the required 20 feet, the tractor would return the contraption back to the starting line.

The first horse was led to the stone boat, but the excited mare didn't want to wait. She pranced and pawed and even jumped in place. As one handler tried to calm her, holding her bit, the other attached the harness to the stone boat. He quickly gave his assistant the sign to let go and then he urged his horse on. The mare dug her feet into the ground as she pulled and strained against the harness. "Yah! Yah!" hollered the handler. The horse tried her best, but she was unable to pull the stone boat the required distance.

The next horse to go was the gelding who had been ridden by the friend of Jim Spencer. Was the horse trained by Mr. Spencer? Heather didn't know. Fortunately for Heather, Mr. Spencer was not in the ring. The young man who had ridden the horse earlier was handling the reins while another young man stood at its head.

As the stone boat was returned to the starting point, the two men brought their horse over to center ring. Unlike the first horse, this one was oddly calm. Heather wondered if the horse had been drugged. She knew Mr. Spencer had used a tranquilizer on Blackjack; maybe he used something on this horse. Or perhaps the horse was exhausted. Regardless, the animal was unable to move the stone boat more than a foot.

"Looks like they didn't condition the horse at all," whispered Chauncy to Heather in a friendly voice. The girl smiled at her mentor. Knowing Chauncy was in a good, competitive mood made her feel so much better. Maybe he wasn't angry with her after all.

The announcer next called Blackjack to center stage. Leading her handsome Morgan to the stone boat, Heather felt a tinge of pride as her horse proudly pranced along in front of his audience. Seeing the stone boat, he momentarily paused and snorted. The big, strong stallion was afraid of the stone boat! He snorted again as he eyed the strange thing. "Oh, Blackjack, don't be silly. You have one just like that at home."

"But his is weighed down with cement blocks, not bags of grain," chuckled Chauncy. "So it looks different. But wait till he gets a whiff of that grain!"

Just as Chauncy had predicted, when Blackjack got within five feet of the stone boat his attitude changed. The horse must have smelled food because he was suddenly willing to get close to the strange object.

Lining her horse up in front of the wood, Heather waited patiently while Chauncy hooked the harness to the front of the stone boat. She gave her stallion a quick kiss on his nose and said, "Be good, boy, and give it all you can. You've got to do this for Chauncy."

Chauncy gave Heather the signal to back away and then, with a simple "Get up!" Blackjack flew into action. His back legs dug into the ground as he pushed against the heavy harness collar. Chauncy stood off to the side, holding the reins, encouraging Blackjack with his voice, and gently slapping the reins on the horse's rump.

Slowly the stone boat started to move. At first it inched forward, and then suddenly, as if propelled by some unseen force, the stone boat appeared to almost glide along the dirt. Blackjack pulled and strained and then, as the weight behind him started to budge, he seemed to have an easier time of moving the pile of grain. Within seconds, the stone boat was dragged across the finish line and the spectators exploded in applause.

Blackjack continued to pull the 500 pounds another foot before Chauncy was able to stop him. "Once he gets going, he doesn't want to stop!" laughed Chauncy as Heather ran up to them. Holding her horse so Chauncy could unhook the harness from the stone boat, Heather praised the Morgan, giving him lots of kisses and even a big hug. Heather was thrilled. Blackjack had done exactly what she had asked of the stallion, and she was so proud of him. Would the other two horses be able to pull the stone boat? Maybe Blackjack had a chance of placing well, even with her screw-ups.

The next horse to go was the chestnut mare who had placed second in the pleasure class. Heather

*Blackjack's back legs dug into the
ground as he pushed against the
heavy harness collar.*

wasn't sure how the horse had done in the other sections of the class, but she thought the mare had placed in the middle of the pack in both races. As Heather watched the mare take its turn, she was amazed at how the horse dug its hind feet deeply into the dirt as it strained against the harness. At the same time, the horse's ears were forward and it looked like she was smiling. Heather was convinced the mare was having a blast.

The horse soon pulled the weight across the finish line and the audience again cheered its approval. The mare's two handlers praised the animal as they all returned to their starting position.

The final horse was the bay stallion who had won the pleasure class and the galloping race, and had placed second behind Blackjack in the harness race. He was a gorgeous horse with a long, flowing mane and a tail that touched the ground. He calmly walked to the stone boat and waited while the harness was hooked. Then, before he was given the command to go, his handler climbed aboard the stone boat, standing on the back edge. Smiling, he told his horse to go, and the stallion obediently burst into action and easily pulled the stone boat across the finish line.

People in the stands laughed and cheered. The stallion's owner waved to the crowd. "That's a real showman," observed Chauncy.

"We'll have the results of the Justin Morgan class in a few minutes," said the announcer. "All exhibitors please stay in the ring."

Heather stroked Blackjack's neck as the entrants stood around, waiting impatiently for the results. She guessed the bay stallion would win the class; he had done so well in every section. If she hadn't been so sidetracked by Annie and Mr. Spencer, then perhaps Blackjack would have won. Chauncy would have been delighted to have a horse he raised win the prestigious class, but she had really managed to mess things up. Blackjack would have done much better in the galloping race and pleasure class if she had been paying attention. Heather never realized how worrying about Annie could distract her so much. Would Chauncy be angry with her for ruining Blackjack's chances?

Heather had promised Nicholas she would tell Chauncy about Annie's past as soon as the class was over. As she wondered what Chauncy would think, she felt cramps in her side and was nauseous. Maybe she didn't have to tell him about Annie. After all, they'd be leaving the show as soon as this class was over. What if—

"This year's winner of the Justin Morgan class is Beaming Bright, owned and handled by Henry Piker."

Cheers and screams of approval shot up from the audience as the big, bay stallion who had so easily pulled the stone boat was led to the ringmaster. His owner, the man who had hitched a ride on the stone boat during the contest, again waved to the crowd. Then, turning his attention to his handsome horse, he placed the long, flowing blue ribbon on the stallion's bridle. The other competitors patiently waited while a photographer took several pictures of the winning team.

"Second place," Heather held her breath as the announcer paused, "goes to Class Act, owned by Helen Dixon and handled by Gary Dixon."

The pretty chestnut mare was led to center ring for her red, second place ribbon. Heather forced herself to smile as she watched. Chauncy would surely be upset that Blackjack hadn't pinned better and he'd be mad at her. Glancing over to her friend, she couldn't tell if he was disappointed. *He is hiding his feelings*, thought Heather. He was going to be so angry.

"The third place horse is Gallant Image, owned by Heather Richardson and handled by both Heather Richardson and Chauncy Campbell." Heather felt a bit of relief as she led her stallion over to the ringmaster. Pinning the long, yellow ribbon on Blackjack's bridle, Heather gave the stallion a gentle slap on his neck and then posed her horse for the photographer. Standing next to Chauncy, Heather put on a fake smile as the flash from the camera went off. Then she silently led Blackjack out of the ring.

"Give him a good rub down and make sure you cool him off well. He's worked really hard today," instructed Chauncy as Heather walked away.

Seeing Nicholas stare at her as she walked toward the barn, Heather felt as if the world were watching her. Chauncy had gone over to his wife and received a big hug and kiss. She could hear him talking with Mrs. Campbell, although she couldn't make out what they were saying. Probably talking about what an awful job she had done showing Blackjack. She continued on her way, head down to avoid looking at anybody.

At the barn, Heather quietly removed Blackjack's harness, walked him around the barn for fifteen minutes, gave him a good brushing, and put him in his stall. She reached into a bag leaning against a bale of hay, pulled out a couple of carrots, and returned to Blackjack. "Here boy, you deserve these."

Blackjack happily ate the treats in record time. Looking for more, he dripped orange goop on Heather's shirt. "One more," decided Heather. "Here you go," she said after coming back with another carrot.

Annie, who was in the next stall, heard the crunch of the carrots and grunted in a low voice. "Hold on, Annie. I'll get you a carrot in a minute." Turning her attention back to Blackjack, Heather told her stallion, "You're such a good boy. And I'm really, really sorry for being so mean to you earlier today. I didn't mean it, Blackjack. Can you forgive me?"

Blackjack rubbed his broad forehead on Heather's chest. Up and down, up and down, harder and harder. "Thank you, Blackjack. And I love you too."

Heather left Blackjack's stall and entered Annie's. Walking up to the mare and giving her a big hug, Heather told her, "We'll be going home soon and then you'll be safe." Annie snorted her approval. "I don't know what to do but I do know that I can't tell Chauncy, I just can't . . ."

"Heather? Where are you?" came a familiar voice.

"Chauncy?" answered Heather, hoping that somehow it wasn't him. "I'm with Annie."

"Oh, there you are," he said as he poked his head into the stall. "Would you come out here for a minute? I think we need to talk."

Heather felt the knot in her stomach return. What was she going to say?

Chauncy walked over to the bale of hay across from Blackjack's stall and plunked his weathered body down. Motioning Heather to join him, he didn't smile, but rather looked serious and concerned.

What am I going to say? What am I going to say? was all Heather could think as she approached Chauncy and sat down next to him. She felt her head pound as she desperately tried to think of some excuse. She did know that she wanted to be as far away from this barn as possible and didn't want to talk to Chauncy. He was going to hate her when he found out the truth, if he found out the truth. She couldn't tell him, she just couldn't.

"Hey, whatcha guys doing?" happily asked Karen as she strolled into the barn.

"We're having a little talk," replied Chauncy in a serious voice.

"What about?" asked Karen.

Heather felt as if she might scream.

"It's between Heather and me, Karen," said Chauncy, in a gentle voice. "We need to talk in private for a few minutes, okay?"

"Sure, Chauncy," said Karen, as she turned and left the barn. Heather watched Karen leave; she wanted desperately to follow her friend.

Sitting next to Chauncy, Heather didn't say a word. It was excruciatingly painful to sit there in silence, but she couldn't simply start talking. Chauncy, however, did know what to say, so after a moment, he again declared, "We need to talk."

"What's up, Chauncy?" asked Heather, trying her best to sound casual.

"I think you know," answered Chauncy, looking directly at Heather.

"What do you mean?"

"I need to know what's going on."

"Going on? I don't know what you're talking about," said Heather, trying her best to lie her way out of losing Annie.

"You haven't been yourself since you came back from the Spring Morgan Show. You've been avoiding me at the barn, and you don't appear to be having fun with the horses. It seems as though taking care of them has become a chore for you. Plus, I've never seen you show Blackjack like you did today. Your mind was elsewhere and because of that you couldn't get a good performance out of your horse. You had a terrible start in the race because you were watching someone or something. Then, in your pleasure class, Blackjack broke at the trot and you normally would have easily prevented that. But you weren't paying attention; that's not like you. Something has been bothering you and I'm guessing it has to do with Annie."

What? thought Heather. *How could Chauncy know?* She hadn't told him anything.

"The problem is," continued Chauncy, "that I've never known you to be dishonest. I'm very concerned about what's going on and the fact that you don't feel comfortable talking to me about it."

"About what?" asked Heather, repeating herself, still trying to deny the fact that she was hiding anything.

"Come on Heather," said Chauncy, a bit of frustration in his voice. "Please tell me what is going on."

"Nothing, Chauncy, I promise." Heather felt trapped and she wanted to escape. Why didn't he believe her?

Annie snorted as she searched her stall for tidbits of hay.

"So," said Chauncy, putting his hands on Heather's shoulders and looking her straight in the eye, "That story you told me about Jennifer McElroy knowing the owner of Annie is true?"

Heather felt her whole body fall apart. How could she lie to Chauncy? "No," she said in a voice so soft Chauncy could barely hear her.

"You made it all up, didn't you?"

"Yes."

"Why, Heather? Why?"

"I'm so sorry, Chauncy. I didn't mean to—"

"Take it easy," gently advised Chauncy as he hugged his friend. "It's okay, really."

And then it all came pouring out. "I didn't mean to lie, Chauncy, really, I didn't. But I found out who Annie really is, and who owned her and, and, and where she lived. She was with Jim Spencer, but I can't let her go back to him, I can't!"

"Slow down, Heather. Slow down. One thing at a time. Who is Annie?"

"Her registered name is Hidden Pond Polly," answered Heather, again in a quiet, subdued voice.

"And who told you that?" asked an unconvinced Chauncy.

"Jennifer."

"McElroy?"

"Yes."

"And how does she know?"

"Jennifer said Annie looks exactly like Polly and she even sent me an old magazine ad with Annie's picture. It's her, Chauncy, I can tell. It's Annie."

"Well, even if it is, why are you so worried? Annie has been sold several times. She may have lost her papers along the way, but she's still legally my horse. She won't have to go back to Spencer's."

"But Chauncy," insisted Heather, "you don't understand. The lady who owned Annie didn't sell her. There was a fire and the horse was never found. Mr. Spencer's assistant trainer said the horse was lost in the fire, but they never found evidence of that. Jennifer told me most people think Polly escaped and the assistant trainer, who hated her, never told Mr. Spencer."

Chauncy bit his lower lip. "That does change things," he told himself. After a moment, he continued, "Assuming this is all true, and I'm not saying it is, who supposedly owned Annie, I mean Polly."

"Jennifer said it was a lady named Mrs. Clayburg."

"That name sounds familiar," said Chauncy. "I think she owned quite a few Morgans at one time, but I haven't heard anything about her in a while."

"I don't know," was all Heather could say. She suddenly felt exhausted.

Pausing again as he thought of what to do next, Chauncy finally said, "I guess the first step is to contact Annie's rightful owner." Then, looking at Heather as he put a hand on her shoulder, he continued, "I hope you'll never keep a secret from me again, Heather. Telling a lie may seem like the easy way out, but once a lie has been told, it has a way of growing bigger and bigger. Pretty soon it gets out of control. I knew something was bothering you shortly after the horse show, and it seemed to get worse every day. You didn't appear to enjoy the horses, and it sure seemed like you were trying to avoid me. Your performance with Blackjack today, and even when you rode Annie for the Maxwells this morning, was well below what you're capable of doing. But I know you didn't do it on purpose and I'm not angry. You were preoccupied with Mr. Spencer being here and I thought it was because of your past history with him and Blackjack. But obviously, it was because you were worried about what might happen to Annie. I understand that, and it's good to love an animal so much that you want to protect her. But you've got to realize that if you had told the truth, we could have worked this out together—"

"But you're going to sell Annie!" protested Heather.

"You're right. I may have to sell Annie, or even simply return her to her rightful owner. That doesn't mean that I want to sell her, but sometimes doing the right thing is also the hardest. If Annie is an unregistered horse, then I can't afford to keep her; and if she belongs to somebody else, I have no right to keep her."

"But it isn't fair," argued Heather, with much less vigor than she had previously shown.

"I'm not saying it's fair. But it is the right thing to do."

Heather didn't speak for a moment. She wiped away a tear, took a deep breath and said, "I'm sorry Chauncy. I won't ever keep a secret from you again. And I'm really sorry for having messed up today."

"It's all right, Heather. I know you were in a tough spot. We'll get through this together, okay?" said Chauncy as he wrapped his arms around his friend.

After a good hug and a pat on the back, Heather felt better.

"Now," announced Chauncy, "I think I need to go find Mr. Spencer."

"Today? Now?" asked Heather.

"I think it's best to deal with this now," said Chauncy as he slowly walked away.

13

SELLING ANNIE?

After Chauncy left, Heather got up and wandered over to Annie's stall. Leaning on the door, she quietly watched the mare eat. There was nobody else in the barn and the only sounds were those of horses snorting, and of a few birds who were nesting in the building. It all seemed so peaceful.

Heather felt much better now that she had told Chauncy the truth, yet she was still worried. Why did he have to talk to Mr. Spencer?

While Heather watched Annie, Blackjack strolled over to his door and poked his head out. "Jealous, huh?"

Blackjack grunted and shook his head. Walking over to her stallion, Heather continued to talk to him until she heard voices. Recognizing one of them as Mr. Spencer's, she urgently slipped into Blackjack's stall. She couldn't face that wicked man.

Heather crouched down against the front wall, effectively hiding herself from anybody who might peer into the stall. Blackjack, curious about his owner's odd behavior, followed Heather to her hiding place and nuzzled her. "Stop it, Blackjack! Stop it!" whispered Heather as she tried to push him away.

But Blackjack thought it was a game and continued to poke Heather.

"This one here?" came the familiar, nasty voice.

"Yes, that's her," replied Chauncy. "She's the one we suspect is Hidden Pond Polly."

"Hmmm . . . I don't know. Head looks the same, has the same star on her forehead. Let me check her back left leg. Polly had an odd triangular marking that was pretty unique."

Heather heard Annie's stall door open and close. She could hear the horse moving around in the pine shavings that covered the stall floor and then, "Lift it up, you old nag."

"Let me do it," offered Chauncy in a much softer voice.

More rustling in the shavings.

"Yeah, that's her, same marking on the foot. I can't believe Kevin lied to me about her, that good-for-nothing kid. Good thing I fired him."

"Well, I think the right thing to do is return Annie to Mrs. Clayburg." Heather bit her tongue when she heard the suggestion. "Do you have a trailer here to bring her to your place?"

"I'm not taking her," replied a shocked and annoyed Mr. Spencer. "I don't want anything to do with this crazy mare."

"Isn't Mrs. Clayburg your client?" asked Chauncy, slightly confused.

"She was, but she sold all her horses last year. Think she's into dogs now."

"Oh. Then do you know how I can get in touch with her?"

"Yeah. I've got her number in my phone. I keep it in my truck which is over by the track."

Heather heard Annie's stall door open and shut and then footsteps wander away. Deciding it was safe, Heather slowly rose. Blackjack, disappointed that the game was over, tickled his friend's stomach. "You silly boy," giggled Heather. It was the girl's first laugh in a very long time.

The next day Heather didn't get to the barn until almost lunchtime. She was exhausted from the stressful events of the show, as well as the long drive home. By the time the horses were safely tucked away in their stalls, her dad had picked her up, and she'd finally slipped off to bed, it was after midnight. It seemed only a few minutes later that sunlight was streaking into her bedroom. Waking up, she momentarily squinted at the bright light, then threw her comforter over her head and fell back to sleep.

"Tired?" asked Chauncy when Heather walked into the barn carrying her faithful dog Champ.

"Yeah. I'm not used to staying up so late," she admitted. "What'cha doing?" she questioned, noting that Rerun was on the cross ties.

"We're going to drive Rerun!" replied an excited Karen as she jumped out of the tack room.

"Really?" asked a surprised Heather. "Is she ready?"

"The vet seems to think so," said Chauncy. "She still has a small area on her back that is slightly raised, and that may never go away, but I'm removing the breeching so there won't be any pressure from a strap pushing down on that area. We should be fine."

"So the harness will look like a show harness," said Heather, mostly to herself, "without the butt strap."

Chauncy smiled. "Yes, and it's called breeching, not a butt strap."

Rerun pawed at the ground and shook her head. She tried to go forward but was stopped by the cross ties, so she backed up instead. Then she moved to the side as much as she could.

"Are you sure you want to drive her?" asked Heather. "She looks kinda frisky."

"Rerun will be fine. She's just got a bit of pent-up energy. Karen, why don't you lunge her for a little while first?"

"Sure, Chauncy."

Heather put Champ into his crate and wandered over to Blackjack's stall. She planned to give him the day off and turn him out in the ring to play, but now she'd have to wait until Chauncy was finished with Rerun. After brushing Blackjack, Heather groomed Annie, Rusty, and Shadow. Finally, she headed to

Frosty's stall. "Let's go for a ride, girl," she told her favorite trail horse.

Heather spent extra time with Frosty, untangling her long tail, picking out her hooves, and clipping the mare's overgrown bridlepath. She was about to spritz Frosty with fly spray when she was interrupted. "We're ready!" shouted Karen.

Stepping out of Frosty's stall, Heather followed Chauncy, Karen, and Rerun to the ring. Rerun already had her harness on and was waiting for the cart. Heather decided to stay at the rail and watch while Karen nervously held her little Miniature Horse's head. Chauncy quickly hooked the harness to the cart and then instructed Karen to step away.

Without climbing into the cart, Chauncy asked Rerun to walk to the rail. The little horse happily obliged. The extra long reins allowed Chauncy to follow from behind the cart, easily keeping up with the horse's slow pace.

Chauncy had Rerun walk along the rail, turn to the right and left, in smaller and smaller circles, halt, reverse, and backup, all things that might cause her pain. But the horse showed no signs of discomfort.

Finally, convinced that all was fine, Chauncy got into the cart. Clucking to Rerun, Chauncy again had the mare walk along the rail, turn, reverse, and halt. Then, Chauncy encouraged Rerun to break into a trot. The mare was happy to go, and pretty soon the pair was whizzing around the ring, with Rerun displaying the amazing road trot that had won her a blue ribbon last year with Chauncy.

Chauncy had Rerun return to a walk and guided the mare to Karen's side. Climbing out of the buggy and handing his young student the reins, he announced, "She's fine. I think we can safely start driving her again."

Karen cheered and hugged her mare.

A few days later, Heather was working Blackjack in the ring when a car pulled into the yard. She didn't recognize the driver, a plump, gray-haired woman, and figured she must be a friend of the Campbells. Continuing to work her stallion, Heather caught a glimpse of the woman as she disappeared into the barn. Who was she?

With her curiosity getting the best of her, Heather decided to learn more about the visitor. She finished riding Blackjack, cooled him off, and led him to the barn.

"I still can't believe they did that," she heard the visitor say.

Heather saw the woman and Chauncy standing next to Annie's stall. "It's hard to believe anybody would lie about the fate of a horse," agreed Chauncy, "particularly to that animal's owner."

Leading Blackjack to the cross ties, Heather tried to appear as though she wasn't listening.

"Well, it is certainly a relief to know Polly is safe. She appears to be very well taken care of here."

"We do love her; she's a very sweet mare." It was then that Chauncy noticed Heather. "Oh, Heather, come here and meet Mrs. Clayburg."

Clayburg? Clayburg! This woman was Mrs. Clayburg? She had traveled all the way from New York to see Annie? Surely that meant Annie would soon be leaving.

"Oh, please, Chauncy. Call me Kathy. Heather, I've heard so much about you. Chauncy tells me you really like Polly."

Heather was embarrassed. "Yeah, she's a neat mare," was all she said as she approached the adults.

"Well, I'd like to thank you for taking such good care of Polly. Chauncy tells me that you've been riding her, and apparently, loving her too."

This woman wasn't at all what Heather had expected. She wasn't mean and nasty; she was nice and friendly. Why, then, had she kept her horses with Mr. Spencer?

"Thanks," said Heather quietly. "Annie is an easy mare to like."

"Do you want to go in her stall?" asked Chauncy.

"No, thanks. I'm not really a horse person, as you can probably guess. I owned several horses for a while, as I thought it would be fun to watch them show, but I had the misfortune of choosing a bad trainer and didn't realize it until it was too late. I've since sold all my horses and returned to my first love, dogs."

As if on cue, Champ barked. He had been napping in his crate, hidden away in the adjacent stall.

"You have a dog?" delightedly asked Mrs. Clayburg.

"Actually, he's Heather's dog," answered Chauncy. "Would you like to meet him?"

"Oh, I'd love to!"

Heather returned Blackjack to his stall and then disappeared into the stall next to Annie's and retrieved Champ. Carrying him over to Mrs. Clayburg, she asked, "Do you want to hold him?"

"Yes, please!" Mrs. Clayburg gently took Champ and cuddled him in her arms. "Aren't you a bundle of sweetness?" cooed Mrs. Clayburg. In response, Champ plastered several wet kisses on the woman. "He's so adorable! What a wonderful dog," she enthused. "I raise Corgis and am actually on my way to a show in Boston today. When Chauncy called, the timing was perfect for a visit here."

"We should decide what to do about Annie," suggested Chauncy.

"You're right. Since you called the other day, I've been thinking about her and whether I want her returned. I did pay a lot of money for her, but then again, she never made much of a show horse.

And if I kept her, that's what I'd want—a show horse. Honestly, because I'm out of the horse business, I really have no interest in owning her. I still have her registration papers, which I brought along with me today; I never had the heart to return them to the Morgan Association after she, she . . ." Mrs. Clayburg's voice faded away. "Anyway," she continued after composing herself, "I no longer have a trainer or a place to keep a horse. What would I do with her? I can see that Polly is truly loved here, and I'm thrilled she has found such a wonderful home. I don't know . . ." the woman became silent again as she reached out and pat Annie on the nose. "You are sweet, aren't you?" Looking at Heather, Mrs. Clayburg could see the anxious expression on the girl's face. Taking a deep breath, she decided, "I don't feel right pulling her away from such a nice home. Still, she was an expensive horse, so I'd expect something in return for signing over her papers. We just have to agree on a price."

"Do you have any idea how much you'd want?" asked Chauncy, hoping it was an amount he could afford.

"No, not really."

"Why don't we go to the house and discuss it over some iced tea?" suggested Chauncy.

"That sounds perfect," agreed Mrs. Clayburg.

Heather watched as Chauncy and Mrs. Clayburg left the barn. Then she brought Annie up to the cross ties and gave her a good, long brushing. She tried to busy herself with thoughts of showing, or of the beautiful foals Annie might have, but her mind kept returning to what was being discussed up at the house. Would Mrs. Clayburg want too much money for Annie? Would Chauncy agree to pay for a mare he had originally taken because she was free?

Time passed slowly but eventually Chauncy and Mrs. Clayburg returned to the barn. They were busily chatting away about the lovely weather New England had been experiencing lately. Hearing their voices, Champ ran up to Mrs. Clayburg, wagging his tail furiously. She scooped the happy dog up and stroked his back as she continued to talk to Chauncy. Finally, approaching Annie, Mrs. Clayburg announced, "I want one last kiss before I leave."

"You're leaving?" asked Heather, surprised that Mrs. Clayburg wasn't staying longer.

"Yes. Chauncy and I have come to an agreement over Polly's purchase price. Now I have to head out to Boston. It's a long ride and I don't want to be late. It was nice meeting you, Heather."

"Chauncy, does that mean what I think it does?" asked Heather.

"It sure does. We're keeping Annie!"

Heather shrieked like a little kid, jumped in the air, and upon landing, gave Chauncy a big hug. "Oh, thank you, thank you!" she told Mrs. Clayburg.

Not wanting to miss out on the action, Champ planted another big, wet kiss on Mrs. Clayburg's cheek.

THE MORGAN MILE

"**H**eather, I think you and I need to have some fun!"

"What are you talking about, Chauncy?"

"Well, things have been a little rough between the two of us lately. Now that everything is settled, problems are out in the open, and Annie is once again a registered Morgan, I think we need to enjoy some good old-fashioned competition. I want to take Blackjack to the Morgan Mile Trotting Races!"

"Trotting races?" asked Heather. "Is that like the Justin Morgan class?"

"No, not really. These races are held on a dirt road in Vermont where Justin Morgan actually raced two New York Thoroughbreds over 200 years ago."

"Cool! I want to go!"

"Great! We'll have a lot of fun, I promise."

"Is it a saddle or harness race?" asked Heather.

"Both."

"Won't that be too much for Blackjack?"

"I was thinking," explained Chauncy, "that I'd drive Blackjack in the harness race and you could ride Frosty in the saddle race."

"I'd love to take Frosty," said Heather, "but actually, I think I'd rather take Annie. Would that be okay? I think it's important for me to show Annie."

"Sure, it's a wonderful idea."

"I can't wait!" exclaimed Heather.

Much like the morning of the Justin Morgan class, the whole gang from Gallant Morgans climbed into Chauncy's truck before dawn, but this trip was different. Heather wasn't nervous or worried at all. Instead, she was as hyper as Karen. Nicholas too, was wide awake and bouncing around as much as his friends. Mrs. Campbell once again brought along a basketful of treats and drinks while Chauncy joked and laughed throughout the drive.

The trip passed quickly and soon Heather and Chauncy were unloading horses. Because the races were being held on a dirt road and not at a racetrack, there were no barns around with stalls to pamper the horses. Animals would have to be tied to trailers and patiently wait their turns.

"Heather, can you help me with this?" asked Chauncy as he climbed into the back of the truck. "I need to get the cart down."

"Sure, Chauncy," replied Heather.

"I'll help too!" volunteered Nicholas.

Soon Chauncy had Blackjack hooked to the cart and walking along the side of the road. There were about twenty horses participating in the day's events and over a hundred spectators present. This was a bit of history being replayed, and many local residents came to watch.

There were twelve horses going in the harness race, which would be run before the saddle race. Six heats would be run, with two horses going in each race. After all horses had raced, the two with the fastest times would race each other. Blackjack easily won his qualifying heat, leaving a long-legged chestnut mare in the dust. When the announcer called out Blackjack's name as one of the finalists, Heather cheered and clapped her approval.

Chauncy was like a little boy, thought Heather. She could tell he was having as much fun as anybody at the event. As he steered the stallion to the starting line for the championship race, Heather got her first look at Blackjack's competition. He would be racing against the beautiful bay stallion who had won the Justin Morgan class. "This is going to be a close race," Heather told Karen. "The other horse is Beaming Bright. He's really fast."

Like the harness race during the Justin Morgan class, this race would start from a trot. With just two horses competing, it was easy for them to trot side by side as they approached the starting line. Then, as the buzzer went off, Blackjack and Beaming Bright flew into action. Heather and Karen jumped up and down and screamed their encouragement to Blackjack.

The two stallions appeared to be neck and neck, and Heather couldn't tell who was winning as they approached a corner and soon disappeared from view. Reaching into a pocket of her pants and pulling out her cell phone, Heather clicked a button, waited for a response, and then shouted into the phone, "Okay, Nicholas, they're headed your way."

Nicholas had walked down to the finish line before the race started so he could have a better view of the winners. "Hold on . . ."

"Well? Is Blackjack in first place?" asked Heather, impatient for any information.

"I don't know. They haven't turned the corner yet." A pause, then "There they are! I can see them!"

"Who's winning? Who's winning?" anxiously asked Heather.

"I can't tell. They're too close," answered Nicholas. "Wait a minute . . ."

"What? What!" pleaded Heather. "I can't stand the suspense. Tell me!"

"It looks like . . . yes! He's winning, he's winning!"

"Who? Blackjack?"

"Is Blackjack winning?" asked Karen, not able to hear what Nicholas was saying.

"Sssh," scolded Heather. "I can't hear."

"Yes! He won!" screamed Nicholas into the phone.

"Blackjack?"

"Yes!"

Heather screamed in delight. "We won! We won!"

"Now take it easy," cautioned Chauncy as he gave last-minute instructions to Heather. "You don't want to tire Annie before the first corner."

"I know Chauncy. I promise I won't go too fast." Heather adjusted her feet in the stirrups, gave Annie a pat, and then urged the horse into a walk. It was time to get ready for their race.

Annie was eager to move into a trot; she could sense something exciting was about to happen. After several minutes of walking through the field behind all the parked trailers, Heather asked Annie for a slow trot.

As the pair made their way around the field, Annie and Heather were called to the starting line. By the time they arrived, a bay gelding, with a rider about Heather's age, was already waiting. "Hi," said Heather, smiling at her competitor.

"Hi," replied the nervous girl.

"When you hear the buzzer, you can start," instructed the volunteer standing between the two horses. "If your horse starts to move out before the buzzer goes off, we'll have to restart the race. Also, you must stay on your own side of the road. You," he said, pointing to Heather, "need to stay to the right, and you," he pointed to the other rider, "on the left. You're not allowed to cross over to the other's side. We have spotters along the road, and if they see you crossing over and getting in the other horse's way, you'll be disqualified. Understand?"

Both girls nodded and guided their horses to the starting line. As Heather was wondering if the buzzer would ever sound, the noisy contraption rang out and Annie flew into action.

It only took a few seconds for Annie to zoom into an extended, ground-eating road trot. The other horse, too, was able to gain speed quickly. Seeing this strange horse just a few paces behind her, Annie decided to go faster and broke into a canter. "No, girl, slow down!" ordered Heather as she pulled back on the reins. Annie resisted the pressure and tried to continue cantering. "No, Annie!" demanded Heather as the horse finally slowed.

Between the fighting and the breaking down into a slower trot, Heather and Annie lost a lot of ground. The other horse had passed them and was making its way around a bend in the road. "Come on, Annie!" encouraged Heather.

This time Heather wouldn't let Annie break into a canter. She knew her horse was excited and wanted to run, so in order to keep Annie trotting, she had to concentrate. The world around her melted away as Heather focused on her horse and the road in front of her.

Annie listened to Heather as they neared the other horse. The mare stretched her legs out, allowing her to cover a lot of ground with each stride. As Annie was about to catch the bay gelding, the horse swung his hind end out into the middle of the road, forcing Annie off to the side, into a ditch. Annie stumbled as her legs hit the dip in the side of the road and threw Heather forward.

Grabbing a handful of mane, Heather was able to quickly regain her balance and keep Annie going, up out of the ditch and back to the race. But again as they were about to pass the gelding, he came over to their side of the road. Trying to avoid the horse, Annie had to slow down and fall back.

"Number 18 is disqualified," yelled a volunteer from the side of the road.

Heather and the other girl both looked in the direction of the voice. "I'm sorry," said the girl to the volunteer as she slowed her horse. "I think Max spooked at something in the grass. Can't we keep going?"

"No, you have to stop. Sorry, but those are the rules."

Heather was as surprised as her competitor. She didn't want to win the race because somebody else was disqualified. That wasn't any fun. Still, she did want to win the championship race so she kept Annie going.

Since the other horse had pulled out, Annie was free to use the middle of the road. There was nothing that could stop the mare now as she picked up more speed and was soon flying past Nicholas at the finish line.

"Yee-haw!" cheered Nicholas.

"We're racing against Beaming Bright?" asked Heather. She had been thrilled when her name was called for the championship race but worried when she saw against whom she'd be racing.

"Yup, looks like you are," replied Chauncy.

"But I thought he couldn't do both the harness and the saddle race."

"No, there's no rule against that," explained Chauncy. "But he's apt to be a little tired by now. Just keep Annie going in that great road trot of hers and you'll be fine." Chauncy held Annie while Heather mounted. "Concentrate on your ride and don't think about who you're racing."

"Okay, Chauncy," said Heather as she and Annie turned and walked away. Reaching the starting line first, Heather looked around. Off to the left she saw the familiar bay stallion. *He doesn't look tired*, she thought.

A few minutes later, the two racers were standing side by side, waiting for the buzzer to go off. Heather grabbed a clump of mane; she didn't want to lose her balance when Annie jumped into action.

Heather licked her lips, took a deep breath, and leaned slightly forward. Then it happened—the buzzer went off and both horses immediately broke into a fast trot.

Annie pinned her ears back as she struggled to get ahead of the stallion, but even with her amazing speed, Annie couldn't get in front of her competitor. The two horses were equally matched and soon they were trotting neck and neck, with neither one able to pass the other.

Heather was afraid to push her mare too hard, fearing the horse would break into a canter. If that happened, she'd have to pull the Morgan back to a trot and they'd lose precious time. Against Beaming Bright, she'd never be able to catch up.

Glancing to her side, Heather could see the stallion's owner leaning forward, trying his best to encourage his horse. The girl realized that he too, was worried about winning. The pressure of the event suddenly slipped away, and Heather smiled. She was in the midst of a fantastic race, challenging a wonderful, talented stallion. She simply wanted to have fun.

Annie felt her rider's tension disappear. She stretched out her legs, grabbing at the ground, inching her way into the lead.

As the racers neared the finish line, people lining both sides of the road began to scream. The horses loved the encouragement, and both continued to trot at high speed, vying for the winning position. But Annie had the advantage with a rider who was relaxed and concentrating on crossing the finish line. Beaming Bright was growing tired and his owner had lost focus.

Annie was now a shoulder's length in front of Beaming Bright and crossed the finish line a split second before the stallion. Standing in the stirrups, Heather raised one arm high in the air. Among all the screams from the crowd, she was sure that she heard Nicholas cheering.

Heather slowed her horse as she searched for Nicholas and found him in the front of a large group of people. She trotted Annie over to her friend. "Congrats!" cheerfully said Nicholas. "That was awesome!"

"Thanks! It was so much fun." Taking her feet out of the stirrups and sliding to the ground, Heather loosened the girth and gave Annie a huge hug. The horse was puffing, her sides heaving in and out as she tried to get her breath. "I better walk her," said Heather as she and Nicholas began the long trek back to the trailers.

*Standing in the stirrups, Heather raised
one arm high in the air.*

Annie calmly followed Heather and Nicholas, head down, relaxed, ears flopping. By the time they reached the starting area, Annie was cool and dry. Her bright, happy expression had returned, and she looked ready to race again.

In a few minutes, Heather and Annie would receive their championship ribbon during a short ceremony the Vermont Morgan Horse Club would hold, but first, she needed to find Chauncy. Heather quickly found the Campbells and Karen waiting for her. "Nicholas, will you hold Annie for a minute?"

"Sure, no problem."

Handing the reins to Nicholas, Heather ran over to Chauncy. "We did it! We did it!" she exclaimed.

"I'm so proud of you, Heather. That was a fantastic race!" proudly exclaimed Chauncy. He gave Heather a big hug and squeeze. It felt so good to be praised by her mentor and she realized that no blue ribbon could compare to the friendship she shared with Chauncy.